P9-BYG-568

NEVER TOO BUSY FOR YOU

MOORESVILLE PUBLIC LIBRARY
304 SOUTH MAIN
MOORESVILLE, NC 28115
(704) 664-2927

F
LUC

MOORESVILLE PUBLIC LIBRARY
304 SOUTH MAIN
MOORESVILLE, NC 28115
(704) 664-2927

NEVER TOO BUSY FOR YOU

Scott R. Lucado

MOORESVILLE PUBLIC LIBRARY
304 SOUTH MAIN
MOORESVILLE, NC 28115
(704) 664-2927

Writers Club Press
San Jose New York Lincoln Shanghai

Never Too Busy For You

All Rights Reserved © 2002 by Scott Raymond Lucado

No part of this book may be reproduced or transmitted in any form or by any means, graphic, electronic, or mechanical, including photocopying, recording, taping, or by any information storage retrieval system, without the permission in writing from the publisher.

Writers Club Press
an imprint of iUniverse, Inc.

For information address:
iUniverse, Inc.
5220 S. 16th St., Suite 200
Lincoln, NE 68512
www.iuniverse.com

Any resemblance to actual people and events is purely coincidental. This is a work of fiction.

ISBN: 0-595-23559-X

Printed in the United States of America

For Irene, who believes.

Acknowledgments

A very special thanks go to Irene, who is my wife and personal reason for knowing that there's a Heaven.

I would like to thank the many others who made this book possible—you know who you are. In particular, special thanks go to Molly Hale and Carolyn Cunningham, two shining examples of friendship. And a final thank-you to Larry Gewax, who reminded me that goals are dreams with a deadline.

Finally, I'd also like to thank all those who've told me that I should write a book.

CHAPTER 1

Of all the things to remember, what I recall most vividly was my house, and how small it seemed. My wife, Sarah, our two daughters, Jessica and Christine, and all our stuff always seemed to be under-foot.

Typically, while walking from one room to another, invariably something—clothes, newspapers, a pair of badly-placed shoes, or some silly toy—lay in wait for me, and would suicidally throw itself into my path, so that I could trip over it, knock it over, break it, scatter it, or be otherwise inconvenienced.

On many occasions, this disturbed my absorbed state causing me to lose my temper just a little, and send the rest of the family running for cover until I got over it. I was no threat to them, of course, but apparently the sight of me snarling, cursing, and venting my petty-tyrant rage was rather intimidating.

I don't think I was ever able to make it clear to them that the most infuriating aspect of my tantrums was that the things I'd trip over were all too frequently my own.

Still, whatever guilt I felt over my grumpiness never got out of hand. My family accepted my shortcomings, and loved me just the same. Maybe they realized that my anger was never at them—only uncomfortably *near* them.

If I was relatively happy, it's because I had a job that I liked, as much as it's possible to enjoy being constrained by labor for someone else's profit. My career, never what I imagined it would be, shambled its way along, with the occasional promotion or cost of living raise to show for my efforts. My employer, an information services company, was not spectacular, offering an imitation of stability in exchange for an imitation of loyalty. Judged by that standard, I was a loyal employee.

Still, each work day had one undoubted highlight, and that was my return home each night. As I drove my sensible sedan along the crowded freeways and down the less crowded but no less hazardous side streets, my thoughts were always of Sarah and the girls. Though the small house was never what anyone would call a center of peace and harmony, it was my home. To me, it seemed as though love radiated from the house in a tangible way, and it drew me homeward.

This routine had its variations, of course. Like all good corporate soldiers, one of the unpleasant realities was that I sometimes had to make business trips out of town. As much as I loved travel with my family, I simply hated these trips. Whenever I was taken away for more than a day or two, I missed the girls and my wife terribly. They felt the same way; their voices over the phone grew increasingly anxious during my absences, though of course Sarah tried her best not to make me feel guilty for being away. She knew it wasn't my choice.

Even writing about this, it seems so mundane that I'm sure many people would define this as being in a rut—a safe and unspectacular routine. If that's what being in a rut means, I wasn't really aware of it. The routine comforted me far more than it upset me—at least, as far as I am able to recall it. Once I turned 40, I learned that predictability was more to be sought than avoided; my body had slowed down enough that the kind of excitement I used to seek seemed more frightening than inviting.

Then on one fairly routine Tuesday morning, as I was headed out the door to the garage, Sarah gave me a routine peck on the lips.

Then the last thing she said to me as I left for work was, "Be careful, honey. I love you."

It was the same thing she said to me every day, but somehow it sounded different that day. Maybe it was because of the light rain that was falling that morning, but I don't think so. She just sounded *different*.

Did she have some way of knowing what was going to happen?

CHAPTER 2

My name, by the way, is Jerry.

I never spent a great deal of time thinking about it, but when I did I considered myself a good man—a loving husband, a dedicated father of my two adorable daughters, a dependable if not overly ambitious worker. I paid my taxes correctly and on time, kept my lawn mowed (though I made only lame attempts at weed control) and my car was always tuned. I never even swore at other drivers. Well...most of the time I didn't.

Part of my life's routine involved going to church almost every Sunday, willingly, if not overly enthusiastically. I admit, I derived a sense of comfort from the sermons. I didn't look too deeply into the messages; the few that made sense made sense, and what didn't make sense I attributed to my own...well, dimness, I suppose, or maybe it was just my inattention to those kind of details.

On the rare occasions when I would discuss religion with anyone, I always explained that I just found it comforting to believe that even with all the evil and unpleasantness loose in the world, there was someone upstairs who had it all under control. That fact wasn't much consolation during really terrible events, but most of the time it was enough.

In terms of personal religious experiences, I never felt particularly close to anything divine, and if only some of what I heard in church made a lot of sense to me, there was definitely something there that I couldn't explain, and that was good enough for me.

So my death at the age of 42 was a great surprise to me.

It came as a flash of bright white light as I was jaywalking across a busy street, trying to run one errand too many during my lunch break.

As usual, Sarah had been right, but I hadn't listened. I should have been more careful.

I can't really describe what it felt like to die. I don't really remember, to be honest. What I do remember of it was that it didn't hurt. I'm sure that my body must have looked pretty bad—it didn't look all that great when I was walking around. Since I literally never knew what hit me, I didn't have to think about it as it was happening. One instant I was *there*, and then I wasn't *there* anymore.

Suddenly I was in a different place. What was different about it wasn't exactly clear—it was just unlike anything that I'd ever experienced before. I don't remember how I got there; I just knew that I wasn't where I had been.

And somehow I knew that I would not ever go back.

A feeling of sleepiness and disorientation engulfed me; I couldn't say how long the sensation persisted. But I drifted off into sleep, and while asleep I had a dream.

In this dream, I was in a small office building, like a title company or a small-business accountant might have. I had a job to do—I knew it was my assignment to accompany someone as he was judged as whether he was headed to Heaven or Hell.

My companion looked like Sidney Greenstreet, and I somehow knew that he was not a nice man—that even though he thought he had fooled a great many people, his number was up. The tropic-weight suit he was wearing wasn't going to be nearly cool enough for where he was headed.

Since I had to process him through the necessary paperwork, we moved into a small room, where he and I stood next to a counter.

Behind the counter a friendly looking middle-aged woman gave me a form; it was a small piece of paper, and I had to write an "x" in a couple of boxes. I don't remember what the forms were, only that I as I was writing, I thought to myself, "Pal, I'm glad I'm not you. Standing there, looking so comfortable and smug, you can't even imagine what you're in for."

With a sense of great self-satisfaction, I handed the piece of paper back to the woman and said, "You know, I'm learning a lot about this place already."

In return, she gave me a puzzled look, so I went on. "I mean, this is an example of something that I thought of as an oxymoron—an efficient bureaucracy. We've got these formalities to observe, yet you're prepared, and now we're all ready. That's great!"

As I finished my little speech, out of the corner of my eye I saw a squad of soldiers approaching. They were dressed in tan uniforms, and wore bandoleers of ammunition crossed on their torsos. Each carried an old bolt action rifle. They moved toward us. I thought they were closing in on the man I was guiding.

It was time for this to come to a conclusion, I thought. The soldiers were about to surround this anonymous condemned man, and lead him off.

That isn't what happened.

Everyone around me—the woman behind the counter, the soldier, and especially my companion, stepped back away from me, and began looking at me with intense concern.

Not knowing the reason for their anxiety, I tried to take a step closer to them. But I was unable to move. My feet were frozen to the floor. Slowly the paralysis moved up my legs and started to affect my entire body.

I suddenly realized, to my ultimate horror, that the man being judged wasn't my companion—it was *me*.

The room fell away from me as I was pulled upward, through the large window behind me. The last thing I remember seeing is the look of fear on the faces of everyone in the room.

But that was nothing compared to the fear I felt within me.

I woke from this dream, gasping for breath. I sat bolt upright, expecting to hear my heart hammering in my ears, but I could feel no part of my body. All I could sense was terror.

As my breathing slowed down, I realized that I was in a very soft bed, much gentler than anything I'd felt before. There was a light smell of potpourri—not overpoweringly, like in the little-old-lady teashops in antique malls, but just a hint of a pleasant fragrance.

A delicate female voice, light and sweet as meringue, whispered, "Jerry, it's time for you to get up."

At first I didn't realize that she was talking to me.

She asked, "Jerry? Are you awake? Please get up. God is waiting to talk to you."

I could see nothing distinct, only an egg-shell whiteness all around me, yet my fear was gradually replaced with a sudden thrill. I imagined that this was still a part of a particularly vivid dream. "God? God who?" I mumbled through my confusion.

The voice became a little less soft. "God. The divine being who runs things around here. You've heard of Him, I'm sure. Now do come along; it's considered rude to keep Him waiting."

Still not quite able to see clearly, and thinking I was in some kind of delirium, I spoke in the general direction of the voice and said, "Gee, you don't think He's mad at me, do you?"

The voice had a hint of mirth as she said, "You'd be a lot less comfortable if He was, don't you think?"

I blinked, and instantly the disorientation was gone. I realized that I must be dead. The whiteness around me didn't diminish, but it came into focus, if that makes any sense.

I stood up.

It was then that I met God.

CHAPTER 3

❀

"Jerry!" A shrill, squeaky, but incredibly powerful voice tore through my consciousness.

After some hesitation I timidly replied, "Lord?"

"Yes, Jerry, it's Me. And just to save us both a lot of explaining, it's really Me, not just some dream you're having or any other kind of hallucination."

"Oh," was all I managed to say.

Perhaps I looked confused, because God asked, "Jerry, are you comfortable?"

I remember feeling that at least I wasn't uncomfortable, now that the fright had passed. I answered Him, "I think so...I'm feeling much better than just a short while ago, that's for sure."

God came nearer, His presence brighter than the brightness around me, and said, "Good. Jerry, are you feeling all right?"

"Now that I think about it, I'm okay, I guess," I answered slowly. "Thanks for asking."

"I'm glad to hear that. I was wondering whether you're up for a little talk," God said to me.

This was all very new and very, very strange, but I figured that I'd better be helpful. Summoning up the tone of voice I would use at work, I replied, "Yeah, sure. I think I can handle that. What would You like to know, God?"

A sound like four thousand fingernails scratching a thousand chalkboards shattered the air. My eardrums felt as though they were being jackhammered. As the screeching slowly receded, I opened my eyes and was beginning to make out some details. I saw a scowling face, neither young nor old, with no obvious indication as to being male or female. For some reason I couldn't help but think of mid-career Joan Crawford.

Then the mouth moved and I heard, "Don't you understand? I'm *God*! I'm here to tell *you* something, you fool."

I hadn't thought of that.

"Thank You," I said.

If this was God, I might not get many more chances to talk to Him, so I wanted to get one thing straight. So I went right to the heart of the matter.

I'd never really understood the purpose of life, and I couldn't help but wonder about the meaning of my death. I figured I might as well ask. "Are You going to tell me why I'm here? I was only 42!" If this wasn't just a dream and I really was dead, I wanted to know why.

The face shimmered and changed, echoing the expression my mother wore when I would ask a really stupid question. God said, "Oh, Jerry, you're just dead. Your body is gone. You're not going to get it back again, and you'll rest a lot easier if you stop worrying about it."

"I guess I can't help it…after all, I've just lost my life! There's a terrific woman and two little girls back there who need me!" I protested.

"Jerry, it is going to take a while," God sighed, "But you'll come to realize that you've gained a great deal more than what you fear you have lost."

"But it doesn't make sense to me," I insisted. I was tired of standing, but it didn't seem as though there was anywhere to sit. Suddenly there was.

God sighed, sank into a comfortable leather recliner that I hadn't noticed was there, and began to explain. "No, Jerry, I suppose it doesn't, really. Sometimes even I forget that when you people first get here, you aren't really aware of what is taking place around you." As God spoke, He became more complete to my vision, as though a wall of wax between us was melting.

I wish I could accurately record what He looked like during that first conversation. But He was more of a presence than an appearance. I mean, He had facial features, but the harder I tried to compare His features to something familiar, the less distinct His image was.

God continued His explanation by saying, "Jerry, for you to understand what has happened, is happening, and will happen to you, you've got to start at the beginning. That's why I'm here to talk to you."

"Do You do this for everybody?" I wondered.

God thought for a bit and said, "Well, not quite everybody, but yes, this is one of My busier activities. You have to realize, Jerry, that a lot of souls were better prepared for the journey you've just made. They've had enough time to think about it, so when they get here, they're really quite content with a quick meeting with Me."

"Really? What do they want to talk about?" I wondered.

"Nothing, really, Jerry. Mostly, they just want to thank Me for letting them in." God smiled gently, almost humbly as He spoke.

Continuing, He said, "Souls such as yours, Jerry, are a different story. The transition isn't quite so easy. You probably don't realize it yet, but you'll come to see that you've been the victim of some very misguided propaganda."

What could He possible mean by that?

"So misguided, in fact, that it obscured your thinking, and made some very simple things extremely complicated," He concluded. "That's very unfortunate, because I have this really great message I try to get across to you, and it keeps getting misunderstood."

"What message is that?" I asked Him.

He smiled a little and said, "You'll see more of what I mean when we have the opportunity to talk some more."

"Thank You," I managed to say. "But whether it's a complicated message or not, if it's from You, I want to be sure that I understand it properly."

"What do you mean by that?" asked God.

Not really sure what He was asking, I said, "Well…you know. Make sense in a…logical way, that is."

God raised an eyebrow about half a foot, tilted His head slightly and said, "Logic? Logic?"

Really feeling unsure of myself, I offered, "Well, yes; a predictable system of order. You know, *if* this, *then* that."

"I know what logic is, Jerry," He said, but still looking a bit puzzled, the Creator went on to ask, "You want a world built on a *system* that makes sense from a mathematical point of view, do I understand?"

"Well, Yes," I replied to God, and thought to myself, isn't that what I just said?

"That's very much what you just said," God reminded me, obviously able to read my mind. "So, you still think that the proper world is a logical world." He glared at me silently for a bit before going on. "To you, somehow logic transcends emotion and chaos and randomness, yes? (Actually, you don't need to answer, since I know what you're thinking, but I also know you're more comfortable with that kind of dialogue mechanism.)"

Okay, I thought, and went on, God, do You want me just to think my responses?

"Do whatever you like, Jerry. You haven't realized yet that you're in *your* Paradise."

I decided, "In that case, I'll speak up every now and then. Thanks."

God nodded absent-mindedly and said, "I'm glad we have that settled. Let's get back to this idea of logic," He continued. "Maybe we can start by you telling Me something. How did you get to be so certain that logic is the most important key to understanding the world around you?"

I had to stop for a moment. That was a good question. As rainbow-colored rain fell in the distance and the raindrops sang out in exaltation, I realized that I'd never really thought about the logic behind my appreciation of logic. It was just something I somehow knew.

My mind started racing; I didn't want to look like an idiot in my very first meeting with God—though something told me it was already too late to prevent that. Still, I tried to think…where had that idea come from? Finally, reaching deep into my brain, I thought of something. "It's…it's what we were taught in school; it's the foundation of social order and the absolute basis of scientific knowledge," I mumbled.

God nodded, with only the top half of His face. "Ah, now we're getting somewhere. 'The absolute basis of scientific knowledge,' you said. That's quite a statement. Please tell Me…what does all this science do for you?"

"Well," I answered slowly, stalling because I didn't have any idea what He was getting at. "Science has given us many useful understandings of the world around us."

"Uh huh," agreed God, nodding with his complete head this time. "I can see that you have a pretty high regard for this kind of knowledge. Still, I'm a bit curious. Have these 'useful understandings' that you mentioned really made your life any better? Longer, maybe, but better?"

I didn't know what to say, so I said nothing. After all, what did I have to compare it against?

God sensed my perplexity and said, "That's fair. Then I guess you'll just have to take My word for it. So let Me explain. There really hasn't been any net increase in the quality of life as a result. Quantity, certainly; your planet is crawling with souls, many of whom are spending longer and longer periods of time writhing around. But My bottom line to you is, not that much has really changed. You humans really aren't any different, and definitely no happier than you ever were."

"Is that really so?" I asked God. That seemed like some pretty disappointing news.

"Jerry," God answered, "Did you ever look around you—I mean really look—at your fellow men? Did you ever notice how happy they *aren't*? Science and technology don't seem to have done much for them. It seems that for every new item of good news, or some small step of what you foolishly call 'progress', there's been at least one bad one for them to latch on to. And their hold on the bad ideas doesn't ever seem to weaken."

I couldn't help but wonder. "So, Lord, if You don't mind my asking, are You saying that science and knowledge and logic are *bad* things?"

"No, Jerry, of course not," God explained patiently. "They're not bad things. Bad is the wrong concept; it sort of implies evil. And these aren't at all evil. They're just *incomplete*. There, you're giving Me that look again, so let Me put it to you simply. You see, as a human, you have lots of pieces. Some logical, some emotional, some spiritual, and many that you haven't even tapped into. But you put too much faith into the separate pieces and not enough into Me. And it's all that misdirected trust that is simply not a good thing."

"I'm not sure I understand," I confessed.

"Let Me put it another way, Jerry," He said. "Those things are small pieces of *something*. But Me, I'm not a piece of anything. I am *everything*."

I felt very puzzled by what He said, and in response God continued with His explanation. "I can tell you're not really sure what I mean, so let Me give you an example."

"I'd really appreciate that," I told Him. "I learn well by examples."

"Okay then, one branch of what you call science, namely algebra, taught you how to find a logical solution to a problem with a variable. Do you remember?"

This example was starting off poorly. I had to admit to the Supreme Being of the Universe that I never really cared for mathematics of any type.

A little exasperated, the Lord Almighty said, "Okay, that's something else you'll have to take My word for. But trust Me, there are mathematical ways of solving problems with several variables. They get pretty tough and abstract and esoteric after a while."

That certainly reminded me of my school years, grinding my way through classes in mathematical theory that seemed even more boring than Sunday School.

Oops. I quickly blurted out, "God, yes, I can see what You're talking about."

After giving me a quick disapproving glance, God said, "Then let Me tell you this, Jerry. Understanding the behavior of you humans is like solving a big algebraic equation with about 5 trillion variables and only a couple of known elements—only harder." Then His face broke into a liquid smile.

Utterly astounded, I gasped, "But figuring that out would be impossible!"

God smiled at me. "For you, Jerry, it would be. But remember who you're talking to." And with that, The Almighty excused Himself and started drifting away, like a leaf pushed by a gentle breeze.

"Wait!" I cried. "Where are You going?"

"Nowhere, really." He stopped and turned toward me. Then He said, with a polychromatic twinkle in His eye, "I'm everywhere, Jerry, always. But I think you need an opportunity to be on your own for a bit. Are you willing to take My word for that? Good. So look around and check things out; this place isn't like anywhere you've ever been—but you'd better start getting used to it. You're going to be here a long, long while. Don't worry, though…you'll see Me again when you're ready. Or maybe even sooner."

Since I was still feeling like the new guy in town, I thought that I had better follow proper procedure. I asked Him, "If You don't mind my asking, when I want to talk to You, don't I have to fill out a form, or ask some angel or something?" I wondered.

God chuckled mirthfully. "Oh, Jerry, you must have seen too many movies, written by some rather dim-witted people who don't have any clue what 'omnipotent' really means. I'm at your disposal; I'm at everyone's disposal. I am infinite, after all. And what is half of infinity? Or a tenth? Or a trillionth?" Then He laughed to Himself, and said softly, "Oh, that's right, math wasn't your specialty."

I appreciated His little joke at my expense, though I couldn't quite bring myself to chuckle along. Even so, it seemed like an awful lot of work for Him. "If You don't mind my asking, God, does that mean You really do everything Yourself? All that stuff about angels…"

"Oh, I do have angels," God corrected me. "In fact, they stay pretty busy doing things that don't require My constant attention. For example, when you first got here, you were woken up by one of My angels."

For some reason, that statement made me a feel a little indignant. "Really? Woken up by an angel, and not by You directly?" I asked.

"Oh, give Me a break," God replied, with a shiny silvery glower on His eyebrows. "You must think I'm new at this. Listen, it's like this. You needed some way of making the transition to this place. If I'd woken you up, you wouldn't have believed it was really Me."

That sounded about right. Even now, I wasn't sure it was really Him.

"It is," He reassured me.

That made me wonder, though, because God seemed so patient with me. If He wasn't too busy, He must have a great deal of help. "Are there lots of angels?" I asked.

"More than a few."

"Do they ever get bored?" I asked. "I mean, if You can take care of everything Yourself, it sounds as though they might not really have a lot to do."

"Oh, there's plenty to keep them busy," God said, once again smiling at my naïve question. "You'll be surprised to learn that a great many folks here feel uncomfortable about addressing Me directly, so they don't. The angels take care of whatever they need."

"But God, if You don't mind my saying, talking to You is…fun, really. You're so accessible. Why would anyone settle for anything less than You?"

After a contemptuous snort, God asked, "You're kidding, right? They accepted a lot less than that when they were alive. Two things seem to hold them back—such minor things, too!—too much belief in bureaucracy, and still more belief in their own insignificance."

I thought about how hard it was to get to see my department Vice President, and said, "I guess You're right. In fact, of course You are. But are there limits on how much of Your time I can have?"

God folded His arms and thought for a moment. "Jerry, I'm not even sure I know what you mean by the word 'time.' Here, the only limits are the ones that you impose on yourself."

I couldn't suppress a laugh. "That's pretty different from what being alive was like," I said to Him.

God looked down at me and said matter-of-factly, "Not really."

As He quickly faded from my view, I heard Him say, "Feel free to talk to Me anytime."

I stood up and wanted to walk around, but I wasn't sure where I could go or might end up, so I sat back down and began to think, or at least I thought I was thinking.

My surroundings seemed pleasant enough, though a little sparse in the way of decoration. Distant scenes faded in and out; wispy fragments of something drifted by, looking like cotton candy being blown by the wind. Cotton candy…that sounded pretty good, and it got me thinking on one of my favorite topics…what's for dessert?

No sooner had the thought entered my head than an ice-cream sundae appeared in my hand—what a blessing! Three flavors of ice cream, with both butterscotch and chocolate toppings. Real whipped cream, too, not that stuff from a spray can. And the maraschino cherries on top tasted just like the ones I remembered from my childhood. It was, in a word, delicious.

I didn't feel full after eating it, and no sooner did I look down at my empty bowl than it was filled by another sundae. So I ate it. It was every bit as terrific as the first one. Amazingly, the one after that was great, too. But by the 27th sundae, I had had enough.

Finally left with an empty bowl, I wondered who did the dishes around here.

So just to see what would happen, I tossed the dish and spoon into the air; as I watched, they turned into a pair of seagulls. Their feathers glittered as they flew away, screeching and laughing as their wings pulsed, taking them God knows where.

CHAPTER 4

Following The Creator's advice, I wandered around, trying to get used to the idea of not being alive. I realized that to the people back on earth, I wasn't me anymore. To them, I had simply left and was no more. But to me, I was still me. I felt the same, or as close to the same as I could ever remember.

Alive, I had certainly been no philosopher. But here, I had to wonder what or who the "real me" had been—was it the part of me that walked around eating cheeseburgers, or was the real me what I was experiencing now, here in Heaven? Or was the answer somewhere in between?

Whatever the answer was, just trying to put the question together in my mind was confusing.

Then in a flash of inspiration, an idea occurred to me. Obviously, my personal experience, while unique to me, was common to everyone here. Perhaps someone already here could help me understand the difference.

And there was one person in particular I wanted to see.

While alive, I had considered myself very lucky that I hadn't had to face the deaths of many people who were close to me. But there had been one that had hit me extremely hard, and that was the death of my father. Dad had died just a couple of years before I did.

Although I felt a little ashamed even to doubt it, I hoped he was here in Heaven. When I thought about it, some of the things he'd done had frequently made me wonder just how far skyward he was going to get. But no sooner had I begun to speculate on his fate than I spotted him walking nearby.

At first, I almost didn't recognize him. He wasn't the older, frail Dad I had last seen in a hospital bed, destroyed by emphysema and diabetes. Instead I saw him as a much younger man, the man he was when I was a young boy. Dad was tall, strong, and eager, walking with the kind of energy and confidence I remembered from a time long past.

Though his image wasn't what I expected, no disorientation of appearance could affect my joy at seeing him. I ran over to cross into his path.

"Dad!" I shouted.

He stopped, and quickly turned to face me. "Jerry…is that you?" It seemed to take him a while to recognize me, as though he had to concentrate very hard in order to see me. I had the sensation that it was a little difficult for him to realize that at last we had become equals.

"It's sure great to see you, Dad." I felt tears rising in my eyes.

He looked slightly uncomfortable as he answered. "Oh, Son, they told me you were coming, but I didn't want to believe them. It seems like I just got here myself." He got a distant look in his eye. "But in another way, it seems as though I've always been here. It's very strange."

I'm sorry to say that I felt a little disappointed. Wasn't he glad to see me? I tried to keep the conversation going. "I know what you mean, Dad. I don't think I'm quite used to the idea myself."

His glance shifted away from me as he said cheerfully, "You will be. Everybody learns to like it here. It really is a nice place. There's lots to see. There's always a good movie showing, and they *really* know how to make a cup of coffee here. And I don't have to worry about sugar substitutes, either." He laughed a little self-consciously.

Of all the things he might have mentioned, that certainly was an odd thing to talk about. "Dad, are you all right?"

Still not looking me in the eye, as though things I couldn't see were distracting him, he said, "What do you mean? Of course I am. It's great finding you. But if you don't mind my asking, did you have any time to think about what this place would be like?"

"What do you mean?"

"Well, Jerry, I spent a lot of time in that hospital, and I wondered how it was going to end...I wasn't even sure when it was going to end. But somehow I knew it would end okay."

"But Dad," I said, more than a little confused, "It didn't end okay. You...went away."

Dad managed to focus his attention a little better. He finally looked me in the eyes and said, "Jerry, I couldn't tell you then, and there was no way you could understand it, but what happened to me *was* okay. In fact, it was better than okay. And now you're here. And that's okay, too, isn't it?"

For some reason, now that he was paying attention to me, I couldn't look directly at him. I simply didn't know what on earth he was talking about.

Then I remembered, I wasn't on earth.

I was struggling to find some common ground when I had an idea. "Dad, what was it like when you got here and you talked with your father?"

"Oh, your Grandpa William? I haven't run into him yet. I often wonder whether he's here at all."

Another awkward pause followed. Finally, he said, "Say, can we continue this conversation some other time? I'm meeting some old friends for lunch. Then we're going to play some football. I'm really pretty good, you know," he said proudly. "I'll see you later, I'm sure. Look me up sometime."

"But how will I know how to find you?" I asked him.

My father didn't answer. Instead, he simply turned away and continued on his walk.

Dad seemed happy enough, and I was glad about that, but his behavior was so strange…so unlike him. No; that's not quite correct. It's more accurate to say that he was unlike who I *thought* he was.

CHAPTER 5

After that odd encounter, for the first time I was beginning to realize what God meant—about millions of variables and what that would mean multiplied by the billions of people on the planet, multiplied again by the billions of other worlds, but somehow I couldn't focus on His words. Maybe He was right—well, of course He was—but it all seemed too abstract and confusing for me to relate to. Maybe I needed something familiar to help me get oriented to my new surroundings.

But even that wasn't really it. I had just seen someone very familiar to me, and he was so different that it was almost worse than encountering a stranger.

I found myself in a downward spiral; the more confused I became, the more confused I felt, which caused more confusion; it seemed like a kind of spiritual vertigo.

Just as I felt I would completely lose my balance, I turned to my left, and there God was, dressed in the most perfectly-tailored wool navy blue suit I'd ever seen.

"Having a little trouble, Jerry?" He asked in His infinitely sympathetic voice.

I was stunned, but His appearance had caused my sense of disorientation to fade. "How did You know?" I stammered.

"Guess," was all He said. Then He sat down, and motioned for me to have a seat next to Him. We were both on a long, luxuriously comfortable park bench. "I prefer for newcomers here to find most things out for themselves, but I suppose I should have warned you about a few things. For example, as you've just experienced, whenever you meet one of your loved ones here, it's not going to be what you expect."

"You're certainly right about that," I said. "Why is that?" I asked Him.

"Well, let's talk for a bit about who they were to you," He began.

I don't remember how it happened, but a lovely park appeared around us. There was a lush meadow in front of us, and off to the right, a small but energetic creek burbled its way across the landscape, dancing past a stand of evergreens. There was a powerful smell of freshness; my eyes tracked a honeybee as she flew towards some nearby clover.

"Jerry, please pay attention," God said softly. I hadn't been aware that I had drifted off.

"Sorry, Lord," I apologized. "So what is it that is so different about people who are here? I don't want any more disappointments like I just had."

God slowly nodded His large head. "Well, Jerry, think about it. What's one of the most different things about being here as compared to where you came from?"

Now that was a poser. "Cheez, God, *everything* here is so different; I'm not sure I could really take a stab at an intelligent answer."

God laughed and said, "Well, that's never stopped you in the past. But let me help you out. The people you knew simply aren't the same as you remember them. For one thing, they never were who you thought they were, and for another, here they become different. You could say that they reach a different state of being."

With that, He extended His arm and opened His hand. It was full of acorns. Before I had a chance to think about it, a squirrel came up and started nibbling on the acorns, casually tossing the husks aside. It was really very pastoral, except that the squirrel was about the size of a dairy cow.

I didn't let that break my concentration, however. "How could these people not have been who I thought they were? Are You trying to tell me that my Dad wasn't really my father?"

God waved His free hand at me in a most impatient manner. "No, Jerry, now you're just being dim. Think about it for a bit. I'll wait."

With that, He froze. His image didn't change; He didn't breathe, blink, or move in any way. He simply remained in place, His hand open. Realizing that this was most likely another of the unusual experiences I was just going to have to get accustomed to, I began thinking about His point. As I tried to contemplate the meaning of heavenly versus earthly life, the big squirrel finished the last of the acorns and bounded off, presumably back to its nest in a *very* large tree.

Yet there I remained, once again drawn back to that maddening question about how different I was from the way I had been. Out of sheer frustration, I was ready to declare that I'd never really been anyone at all, except for the fragments that I had allowed other people to see.

Instantly, God patted me on the knee. "Exactly," He said.

"What?"

God sighed. "You've found the answer without even realizing it, Jerry. Think of all the different sides of yourself that you showed to the outside world. Jerry the father, or Jerry the employee, or Jerry the neighbor. Let's not forget Jerry the husband, of course. I *wish* I could forget Jerry who was a little too friendly with young women."

I knew He'd bring that up sooner or later, I thought guiltily to myself.

"So," He continued, "Which of these Jerrys was the real one? Do you even know yourself?"

I couldn't stop myself from feeling a little defensive and saying, "Well, the part about the young women wasn't really a big deal, you know."

"Yes, don't worry about that," God said forgivingly. "If you'd done anything to hurt that wife of yours, you'd know about it by now. So it's safe to say that wasn't much of the real you. But who was?"

"I don't know, Lord," I said. "I guess each was part of me, in some way. I certainly didn't let my whole personality be seen by the whole world."

"Why not?" God asked.

"That's a good question," I said, though thinking to myself, He's got to be kidding. As soon as that thought flashed through my head, God scowled at me. Another oops.

"Good Lord, was I supposed to talk the same way to my boss as to my wife or my kids? Each relationship was different."

God rested His chin on His left hand. "Are you telling me that you, and all the people around you, had different roles, and that affected your behavior?"

That about summed it up. "Yes," I said.

"Okay, Jerry, I can understand that," God answered. "But let Me tell you something. Here, there are no such roles. You—and those around you—are able to be their true selves."

"But God," I protested, "I'm trying to tell You that I'm not even sure who my true self is."

God stood up and motioned for me to stand as well. He swept His arm around and said, "Jerry, you have all of this to help you. And however long it takes you, you can find out. Remember, you're in Paradise."

"What's that got to do with it?"

"Well," He said, looking and sounding just a bit irritated, "It means that you, like the people you will encounter, will always feel great, no matter what happens. Take your Dad, for instance. He may not have looked like it, but he was truly glad to see you. What you can't appreciate, though, is that he was already glad. And he'll keep being glad, no matter what."

I still felt a little hurt—though to be honest, not very. "But he just kind of blew me off!" I reminded God.

God goose-necked His face closer to me with a very reassuring look and said, "Jerry, don't you see? He knows he can't hurt your feelings, or give you anything, or take anything away, so he doesn't worry about it. Everyone here is like that."

"But it isn't just the way he treated me, God. He seemed a little confused, almost like he's uncomfortable with himself," I told Him.

Nodding, God said, "Very perceptive of you, Jerry. I know that you and your father were quite close, though, so I'm not surprised you noticed it. As a matter of fact, he is as you have described him."

"Is that part of who he really is? Just a confused man who likes to drink coffee and watch movies?"

God smiled patiently and explained. "Jerry, he's still going through a lot of what you're going through. He's moving along on the journey of trying to find who he really is. It's going to take him quite a while, partly because he was never as introspective as you have always been (even though you never thought of yourself that way). He was too busy working to give himself the luxury of self-examination." Then He held up a hand to keep me from interrupting. "There's no rush, of course. Your father has every opportunity to work it out, and I mean that quite literally. But there is more to it than just his personal journey of self-discovery."

"Such as?" I asked, once again not understanding what God was trying to tell me.

God looked away from me, as though He didn't want to speak the words He was about to say. "This isn't going to be easy, and please don't take it the wrong way. So let Me just put it to you this way, Jerry. Imagine how you would feel if you turned around right now and saw your wife. What exactly would you be able to say to her?"

"God..." I started to say, but stopped, unable to continue. It was just too horrible to contemplate. Sarah, taken away too? My surroundings started fading into a velvety gray, indistinct and distressing.

At last I said, "I see. Poor Dad."

After that, I needed to sit back down. Fortunately, the bench hadn't faded away with the rest of the scenery. I sat quietly for a while, trying hard not to let the sense of loss overpower me.

God stood nearby, looking towards me but not quite at me.

"You know, God..." I began, as I lifted up my head.

"Yes, I do," He interrupted, with a comforting smile.

I smiled in response, and continued. "...My Dad and his father were never very close—in fact, they really didn't agree on very much at all. But why haven't they spoken?"

The Creator of Everything looked very serious. "To be blunt about it, Jerry, your father isn't sure he wants to see his dad. When he makes up his mind, he'll see your grandfather."

But there was another part of the problem that concerned me. If my Dad had been a character—and he was, believe me—his father was a great deal more uncontrollable. I couldn't stop myself from gently asking, in a whisper, "But is my grandfather even here?"

God shrugged His enormous shoulders and remained silent.

I didn't understand. Sensing my puzzlement, God sighed and said, "Look, Jerry, it's like this. Whether your grandfather is actually here or not doesn't make any difference."

"You mean, my Dad would just see his father as a kind of illusion?"

God nodded slowly, as though surprised that I had figured that out on my own. "Not exactly, but that's close enough for now. If your grandfather isn't really here, your Dad would create the image of his father that he'd need to see. Maybe I'd ask an angel to stand in for your grandfather for a while. Whatever it would take to keep your father happy."

That made some sense, even though it gave me an uneasy doubt. "My Dad wasn't an illusion to me; he was real," I told God hopefully.

"Was he?" He answered, in a manner that wasn't exactly comforting.

I felt a shudder through my being. "Oh, please don't tell me that."

Then an idea occurred to me. I said, "Wait a minute...I wouldn't imagine my father treating me like that. So there, that was really him."

"Sure," said God, His lower lip drawn into a tight smile.

"God, I have to be honest. Although I don't exactly feel bad about it, it is kind of a let-down," I confessed.

"Yes, Jerry, I know it seems that way to you," He said as His eyebrows took on a reassuring furriness.

I was curious, though. "Can You tell me more about why it's like that up here?"

"Not just yet, Jerry." He said. "We'll talk about this some more, later, after you've had the chance to learn more for yourself." He started to fade away, like evaporating steam.

CHAPTER 6

Before He disappeared, I waved to Him and said, "God, before you go, I have another question."

God's face broke into a grin that almost seemed self-conscious, and His appearance re-solidified. "I know you do, Jerry. You want to know why different parts of My face keep moving."

"That's right!" I was still impressed by God's awareness of everything.

God's face relaxed as he started to explain. "You know, one of the things I've always thought was most interesting about Me is My ability to make any part of My being move independently. I mean, of course I can, right?" He winked at me, as though we were sharing a private joke. "But as you can imagine, that's not the sort of thing I want them to write about in scriptures. It can give people the creeps. You know, when I was younger, I was great fun at parties...yes, parties, believe it or not. I used to entertain souls endlessly by contorting My face into funny expressions, doing impersonations of people who never made it to Heaven—politicians and lawyers, mostly. But then it got kind of crowded up here, and I figured, why bother?" God's concluding sigh sounded almost like He was sad about it. The He looked up and said, "If My facial expressions make you uncomfortable, just let Me know; I can stop."

"No, that's okay," I answered unconvincingly.

God smirked and said, "Now, Jerry, don't you know it's all right for you to speak your mind? I can't expect you to like everything about Me, at least not yet. I know perfectly well that I take some getting used to."

"Well, okay," I answered sheepishly. "But I really am starting to like it around here."

Then, hoping to change the subject, I looked around at the nearly empty landscape, such as it was, and said, "You know, You were talking about crowds, but I hardly see anyone else at all. It doesn't *seem* crowded here."

God sniffed and explained, "Not to you, it doesn't. This is *your* Heaven—you're content with everything around you. I'm the one who has to deal with crowd control. But really, it isn't like this is some cruise ship, where people have to jockey around, worrying that we'll run out of deck chairs. This is Heaven. There's plenty of room; as much room here as there is love from Me."

"So what do You mean by crowd control?" I asked.

"Well, that's how I refer to one of My main jobs, listening to all the requests," He told me.

"What requests?" I wondered, looking around, trying to see whatever might be there, but not finding much.

"The ones you people are constantly making," He said, frowning. "And endless stream of this sort of thing: Fix this; give that; reassure my widow; tell me what's going on; appear there; restore so-and-so's faith; give me a pet—no, not that kind, a different pet; tuck me in; let's go for a walk; tell me about life on Mars; why did You flood my house twenty thousand years ago; can I please go back?...It never ends."

"You mean, You answer prayers, even from people up here?"

"Jerry, get a clue," God snorted. "I *listen* to prayers; that's My job. *Answering* them, no matter where they come from, is a different question altogether."

"Do You answer them all?"

God appeared to relax a little and said, "Up here, sure I do. I have an obligation to keep everyone happy. But in case you're wondering—and I know you are—for those who are still wrapped in physical bodies, it's a very different story."

"In what way?" I wondered, still amazed at His ability to anticipate me.

"Let's look at it this way, Jerry." God straightened up and I saw that He had suddenly transformed Himself into a stereotypical college professor, complete with mortarboard. "Suppose you pray for your neighbor to get hit by a car," He said, His hands folded like a pious schoolboy.

"I'd never do that!" I protested, straightening up in indignation and shock.

God smiled patronizingly and responded, "Well, yes you would, Jerry, and in a way you did—only much worse. But anyway, work with Me on this. Suppose—just for now—that you did, and suppose your neighbor was simultaneously praying for *you* to get hit by a car. Whose prayer should I answer? Yours? Hers? Neither? Both?"

I had to laugh. "Judging by the outcome, I'd have to say You answered my neighbor's prayer."

God shook His ears and smiled. "Well, Jerry, I guess that wasn't a very good example. (You may find this hard to believe, but even I have trouble explaining things sometimes.) Your neighbors actually liked you quite a bit, and are very sympathetic toward your widow and the kids. Remember that bachelor up the street, Mike? He feels particularly bad for Sarah—he'll be paying her a friendly visit soon."

Sarah? That cheeseball loser Mike was interested in Sarah? I frowned and couldn't stop myself from saying, "I'm not sure I like the sound of that."

"It hardly matters now," God sighed, dismissing my concern. "I'm trying to tell you that I can't always answer every prayer…and," He said, once again holding up a hand to prevent me from speaking,

"Before you start arguing with Me—I've never felt a particular obligation to do so."

With that He folded His arms and was silent. I recollected some of my own prayers, and I felt embarrassed by their selfishness and shallow greed. After a realization like that, I wasn't about to disagree with The Almighty.

Especially with Him standing right in front of me.

Breaking this uncomfortable silence, God finally spoke. "The vanity of people is incredible, even to Me—vast swarms all eagerly and stupidly pursuing their own way until they stumble, and then expecting Me to just drop everything and sort out their little problems," He pronounced.

That reminded me of something I'd once heard when I was alive. "You know, I think someone said that people take too much credit for the good things in their lives, and too little blame for things that go wrong."

"You don't know the half of it, Jerry," God said, nodding in agreement, but sounding sad. "What I want is to teach you, all of you; if only you knew how to learn."

"What kind of lessons?" I asked, wondering what kind of school God would set up.

"The kind you can't learn from TV, that's for sure," God said. "Do you remember your old friend Maggie?"

Maggie! I hadn't thought of her in a long time, but suddenly the memories of my friendship with her came flooding back. She was a truly wonderful woman, and one of the most special friends I'd ever had. When I was just a shy and very insecure adolescent, Maggie had introduced me to a whole world of possibilities. I remember her laugh—no schoolgirl giggle , but completely honest and forthright. And she always had a ready smile; not just for me, of course, but for everyone she came across.

She died of cancer when she was just twenty-seven.

When that happened, I cursed God mightily, sickened and furious that someone so wonderful would so quickly and unjustly be taken away.

Remembering my anger, I said to God, "What about her? Is that Your idea of a lesson? That was a horrible time for me, and I don't even want to think about what it was like for her family. For all Your might and power and wisdom, couldn't You have come up with some easier way to teach us whatever it was we were supposed to learn?"

God took a deep—and I mean deep—breath, as though inhaling skies full of air, clouds and all. "I guess we'd better talk about Maggie some other time. But just so you know, the lessons aren't all quite so stark, Jerry. There are all kinds of them, and they are everywhere. Unfortunately, you just choose to ignore the easy ones, so you really leave Me no choice but to teach some things the hard way."

I wasn't exactly sure what He meant.

"Oh, all right, let Me give you a basic one," God sighed impatiently, as though talking to a rather simple-minded tree. "Here's one you should be able to understand: Birds eat worms, then they die and worms eat them."

"Oh, ashes to ashes, You mean," I interrupted. Nothing hard about that, I thought to myself.

"Yes there *is*," God insisted, sounding more than a little frustrated. "You think you are so comfortable with the predictability of that cycle. Be born, grow up, reproduce, get old, become a grandparent, die."

"Well, I guess that's the way it is for most people," I said, even though I hadn't quite made that cycle myself.

Pointing a delicate finger upward, He said, "Listen to Me carefully, Jerry. Maybe that is the basic story for many, even for most, but not for all. There has to be some variation. Because *life itself is variation.* I love the variability of what I've created; the elements that you (rather narrow-mindedly) call 'randomness' and 'unpredictability.'"

God had a faraway look in His eyes, the way a teenage boy looks after he's finished reading brochures for new cars.

"I guess I wouldn't like it if everything were the same..." I muttered, trying to sound agreeable.

"*You* wouldn't like it?" God growled. "You wouldn't even exist at all!" He snorted. "Why would I need a Jerry, or humans, or any living creatures, if I was content with sameness? That whole business of the world being 'without form, and void' would include you, friend Jerry. I made you so that I'd have something to do."

I hadn't thought of that.

"No, you sure hadn't," God confirmed with a nod of His substantial head.

It took a moment for it to sink in. The fact that I had been alive seemed to me to mean that I had *taken for granted* some sort of right to exist, and my presence here seemed to say that I even had a right to continue to exist, in some form.

"Don't be so certain," God said, not for the last time. "Taking things for granted is a real problem for you."

"So, what's the alternative, then?" I asked in response. "Don't we get a vote in anything? Do we just tumble through our little lives, being born, living and dying for Your amusement?"

After a brief pause, God said, "Well, yes, that's one way of looking at it."

"What!" I protested. "That can't be right!"

God explained a little, having expected me to be upset at His response. "It's not that simple, of course. Nothing is ever *that* simple. Maybe sameness is simple, but I just said I don't like sameness."

I was a little irritated by this. "So just how is it?"

God sighed and very slowly said, "You're like...children in a way."

Great. "And you're the Heavenly Father, is that right?" I said, almost angrily. I hoped God wasn't going to use more old metaphors.

"Yes I am, Jerry, and I'll use whatever metaphors I like," He said in His matter-of-fact way. "But I'm in no hurry. Let's hear your side of it. You have children. *Why?*"

Although it had seemed like a good idea at the time, I couldn't recall why exactly I had had kids. I answered with the first explanation that came into my head. "Geez, God, if we didn't have kids, that would kind of be the end of us, right?"

God shook His head like a dog—and His ears wobbled like a basset's. "Sorry. That's rationalizing at worst, and philosophizing at best, not your true personal reason, Jerry. Think about it a little longer."

After standing there like an idiot for a while, I shrugged my shoulders and admitted, "Well, then, I guess I don't really know why I had children."

God smirked a little and said, "You're right. You don't really know. So I'll tell you. Like most humans, you did it out of a form of vanity, as a way of perpetuating yourself. You also wanted to earn the admiration and envy of others, by having perfect-smart-beautiful-wonderful kiddies."

It bothered me to admit it, and I was too proud to say it out loud, but that seemed about right.

"Of course it's right," God reminded me. "Now, you don't have to answer this next question, but were they always perfect, smart, beautiful and wonderful? Or were they ever flawed, dim, unappealing and irritating?"

I knew that He knew the answer, and I didn't want Him looking at me while I thought about it. There were many times when I'd lost my temper with my daughters, even though I adored them. I looked away from God and glanced down, at a floor that wasn't there.

God nodded in agreement with my thoughts and said, "Sure. Relax, Jerry. You knew that your prime responsibility was to nurture your children—raise them to be good people, contributing members of the community. And you knew that while you weren't perfect, you wanted to do your best to raise them right."

Defensiveness crept up on me. "I guess that was a mistake, too, You're going to tell me?"

"No, not at all," God chuckled. "It was absolutely correct. But even you, a lump of flesh, knew that you couldn't expect them, or want them, to do things they weren't ready for. Did you let your oldest drive the car when she was six years old?"

"Don't be silly," I scoffed.

"She asked you, though, didn't she?" God insisted. "And wasn't she pretty upset when you wouldn't let her? She didn't understand your explanation, did she?"

"No," I replied. "But just because it made her unhappy didn't mean I was going to let her have her way." I spoiled both of my little girls, definitely a lot more than I should have, but not that much.

"Oh, I see," God said, nodding slowly. "Yet somehow you think that your relationship with Me is different. What if you are wrong?"

Suddenly I felt very, very small, as though I was a newborn. My surroundings were totally unfamiliar but I felt no fear; everything I could sense around me seemed new and clean and shiny and safe and wonderful.

"Jerry," God whispered gently in my tiny ear, "What's the difference between good and evil?"

For some reason I couldn't understand the question. I could make out the individual syllables, but nothing made sense. "Aaaah, uhh," was about all I could say. I wasn't uncomfortable—just a little dizzy. I really had a craving for some warm milk.

God looked at me, seeming like the only creature in the universe. "Dear Little Jerry, if I explained the difference to you, or even the difference between up and down, do you think you could understand it?"

I couldn't respond, and soon I lost my ability to concentrate at all. Somewhere behind God's left ear, I saw a large blobby pink thing that bounced slowly upward, as though rolling up an unseen staircase. I waved my stubby arms at it and solemnly stated, "Yuuh."

God smiled and said softly, "This is how I see you, Jerry." Then His voice hardened as He continued. "You are petulant, inarticulate, incapable of understanding anything. It's okay, because that's how I made you. But you, through your whole life, learn just about exactly the same way that your children do—only more slowly."

Suddenly I found myself back in my original form, feeling more ignorant than ever—and the thought of warm milk was not at all appealing. "So, what You're saying to me is that much of what happens to us is really lessons?"

"More or less," God agreed. "Your ability to learn is one of My greatest gifts. But if I made all the lessons easy, would anybody learn anything?"

I tried to explain it to Him. "There is so much happening around us, all the time; we can learn from what we see, without needing to be hurt. Learning can be fun."

"In what way?" The Almighty asked. "Can you learn agriculture from watching bees gather pollen? Parenting from watching a frog lay eggs? Life has some realities to it that I intentionally made tough. This may be news to you, but fun is supposed to be a reward, not a way of life."

"Why would that be so bad?" I shot back. "Why can't we all have fun all the time?" The questions formed in my head and were out of my mouth before I had the chance to realize that I had started whining just a little.

"You can certainly try," God answered. "Many of you do. It's like having a diet of nothing but desserts. How well do you suppose that works?"

I thought of that 27th ice cream sundae, and blinked. When I opened my eyes, God was nowhere to be seen.

CHAPTER 7

Of the many strange things that I learned about life in Heaven, one of the strangest is how I began to feel about those I left behind. My wife, Sarah, and I had been very close—we were, in fact, really rather proud of our marriage.

And my daughters…well, it really is no exaggeration to state plainly that they meant the world to me. I remember rushing home from work every day just to see them; even as they began to grow up and realize that their father was just some goofy guy, not the wisest, greatest man on earth.

To put it another way, of the things I loved about being alive, my wife and daughters truly were the brightest lights of my life.

When I died, though, that light was simply extinguished. Snapped off, like throwing a switch, a single anonymous switch on a panel of millions upon millions of switches. And while I recognized and acknowledged a hollowness in my spirit, I would be lying if I said that I actually missed them, in the way that I missed them when I was away from home on a business trip.

Here, I slowly began to realize that I was freed from so much of what I had had while alive. I didn't feel liberated from it, only separated, the way you feel separated from your hair after you get it cut. About all you can do is look down at the floor and sigh…if you even do that much.

That's an odd thing to say, I know, and it was far stranger still for me to come to accept it. After all, one of the first things I did when I arrived here was look for my father—yet it seemed as though I had no such feelings for the living.

And no feelings of guilt about it, either. That seemed especially unexpected. With the religious upbringing I had been given as a child, guilt was always present—at an absolute minimum, we had it hammered into us even to feel guilty about having nothing else to feel guilty about.

Since I arrived here, whenever I think of my family, and I recall events from our past, the only real sensation is an absence of feeling, not so much a numbness as indifference, frankly, like watching a soap opera in a foreign language.

Feeling this way didn't really bother me, since I wasn't really feeling anything at all, but I decided that I needed to talk to the Big Guy about it, just to make sure I wasn't missing something—or worse, doing something wrong.

I held my arms outstretched and spoke softly. "Please, God, if it's not too much trouble...could You explain something to me?"

In a flash—and I mean that literally—God appeared and said, "Hi, Jerry. Something on your mind?"

As if He didn't know. "Well, actually, Lord..."

"Wait," He said, waving His hand at me, "Before we get into that, let Me tell you something."

"Yes?"

"For future reference, Jerry, whenever you want to talk to Me, you don't have to make a big production out of it."

I felt a little embarrassed. "Really? What exactly was I doing?"

God frowned slightly and said, "Well, frankly, you were invoking Me, like you were Merlin and I was a dragon or something. That's not necessary. In fact, I really don't care for that kind of treatment."

Taken aback—literally, because I took half a step backwards—I asked, "Do You mind telling me why that is?"

God took a deep breath and started to explain. "Jerry, the whole time when you were alive, there was a kind of separation between you and Me."

"Separation?"

"Well, sure," He said patiently. "You were there, in that space and time, and I was…excuse Me, am here, outside of space and time."

"Meaning what, exactly?"

Luckily God was in a good mood, because He didn't display any irritation with my dimness. "Jerry…you're here now, too. That's what being in Heaven means; you're a part of all that I have to offer. So if you're wondering whether you can talk to Me for a little *time*, remember that the notion has no relevance here. Just think of Me, and I'll be here."

"Thanks, God, I'll try to keep that in mind," I said cheerfully.

"Please do," He replied. "Now let me see if I can tell what's bothering you." With that, He looked me over, the way a butcher scans a side of beef. "Oh, you're wondering why you aren't more concerned about the folks back there. Pretty common question, actually."

"As usual, You are right," I said encouragingly.

God raised His right eyebrow and said in a voice laced with sarcasm, "It's good to know that you approve."

Sufficiently humbled, if not humiliated, I thought about making some comment, then decided I'd better be quiet. God's eyebrow lowered in slow acknowledgment.

"Well, let Me ask you a couple of questions," He said. "You don't object, do you?"

I let Him have His little joke.

"So," He continued, "Since you've gotten here, how many times have you been hungry?"

I wasn't expecting that kind of question. "Well, I ate all those sundaes," I told him.

"True," He confirmed, "But not because you were hungry. So tell Me, then, how thirsty have you gotten? Or sleepy? Or angry? Have you even noticed that there aren't any bathrooms around here?"

Sure enough, there weren't…and no, I hadn't noticed until He brought it up.

"There's a reason for that," God said, tapping me on the left shoulder. "It's because they're simply things that you don't need here. Appetite was necessary for nourishment—but here, I give you all the nourishment you will ever need."

"That's very considerate," I said politely, "But what has that got to do with my feelings…or my non-feelings, really?"

"Ah, Jerry, all that you left behind, and I mean all of it, just doesn't have a place here. And it strikes you as odd, but that includes the people you loved who are still there."

I thought about that for a bit. If that's the way it had to be, then okay, but why that particular way?

Anticipating my question, God said, "For now, you may just have to take My word for it (and please do; you have no idea how many have mis-taken My word), but I made it this way because if it were any other way, this would just not be a very happy place."

Nodding in agreement, I said, "I can picture a place with everyone feeling lost and abandoned, like homesick college freshmen."

God smiled a little. "Well, it wouldn't be all *that* bad. Some of you would like it here anyway. A lot of your fellows were quite happy to be set free from a life that had grown wearisome. Here, their sense of relief is pretty profound."

"I hadn't thought about that," I admitted.

"No, you didn't," God said, "Just one of the many things you haven't thought about. But you're right in the sense that too many people, such as yourself, would wonder about the seeming injustice of their deaths, and I don't even want to talk about it. Because that is the path that leads to…questioning My judgment. Ugh."

"Do people do that?" I asked in astonishment.

God's face turned hard as stone. "Don't trifle with Me, Jerry. You've done it yourself plenty of times. And before you say anything to try to defend your foolish self, let it go."

"If I can ask one more question, though," I asked quickly, hoping to change the subject, "Do they…still have any feelings for me? I mean, do they miss me?"

God got a very solemn, almost sad look on His gentle face. "Jerry, you don't need Me to find the answer to that question."

"What do you mean?" I asked.

"Didn't *you* miss the people you loved who died? In fact, don't you still?"

With that, I knew what He had been talking about. Absence of feelings or not, I hung my head and began to cry.

God, in His mercy, was kind enough to leave me alone for a while.

CHAPTER 8

Experiences like that made me realize just how much it takes to get used to Heaven. You have to learn to be careful about your thoughts, since they have great power here, and you quickly cross the line between amusement and discomfort.

But with just a little practice, it's fairly easy to do many entertaining things. I had always wondered what it would be like to fly, so I tried that for a while—and this being Heaven, I didn't have to worry about slamming in to nasty things or hurting anybody, least of all myself. I have to tell you, it was such a blast! I soon discovered that I could go as fast and as far as I could imagine going.

This led to more experiments. I wondered what it was like to be a cloud; soon I became a magnificent strato-cumulus, stretching for miles. I looked down upon fantastic landscapes in which multi-colored rivers ran up into mountains. Then I rained for a while on a desert and watched lush greenery sprout from gray sand.

Creating was fun, but I have to say that destroying had its own pleasure. On one occasion, I carefully built up a continent, tugging mountains up from nothingness, and filling in the details, like forests and lakes. Once it was done, it was a lovely sight to behold. Nonetheless, I ravaged it with earthquakes and tornadoes, wiping it clean and finally bringing down an enormous firestorm that turned the entire landscape into glass.

Then I shaped the molten glass into an ornate paperweight before realizing that I didn't have a desk to put it on. I tossed the paper-weight into the sky, where it mushroomed into an enormous gossa-mer umbrella before fading away.

Things happened at my whim; I wondered whether whoever or whatever was watching me thought of it as being hopelessly unpre-dictable.

Every now and then, I saw God in the distance, looking hurried, but He always looked me with His knowing smile. I smiled back. It seemed like the polite thing to do.

It didn't bother me much to have God appearing and disappear-ing, but suddenly it made me think that my family must have thought of me the same way—simply vanishing without any reason.

But I would never reappear. In the end, my death wouldn't mean much; just a number on a tally sheet in a file on a desk in an office in some anonymous government department. If I was lucky, maybe they'd put a stoplight at the intersection near where I had died.

"God?" I asked of empty space. "Are You busy?"

"Never too busy for you, Jerry." God suddenly stood before me and smiled at me in that way He has of conveying concern, patience, and infinite nurturing.

I started to speak. "I'm beginning to understand the idea of life being about learning, but I have to confess that I'm not convinced. There's just so much suffering in the world; so much hardship. You could put an end to it. Why don't You?"

After a long pause and a heavy sigh, God replied, "I get that ques-tion a lot. Now look, Jerry, when you were alive, you were glad that there was shade, weren't you? Wasn't it nice to get out of the bright light?"

I shrugged my shoulders and said, "Sure."

"Did you think it was evil or unnecessary for there to be dark-ness?"

"No, not really. It came in pretty handy at night."

God smiled and said, "Well, Jerry, life is kind of like that. Sometimes it just needs to be dark." And that was all He had to say about it.

I frowned and said, "Excuse me, God, but it's a long leap from sitting in the shade of a maple tree to the thought of a massive famine…With all due respect."

God's face suddenly looked very, very tired. "I knew we were going to get to this. So, you want to criticize Me? Pass judgment on My plans? Do you think you could be a better Divinity than I am?" Everything around me started to change in color to a kind of strangulated purple. There was a distinct smell of burning toast.

"No, that's not what I meant." I shrank away a bit.

"Don't lie to Me," God snarled, speaking very slowly. His eyes glowing with an amber fire. "You think you know what's going on, and that you'd be better at it. You people are all the same! Every time you get some specific attention from Me, do I get any thanks? No! All I get is whining. 'Gee, God, You gave me talent but no money', or 'What am I supposed to do with all this education?' or 'What's the point of being such a great athlete if I can't get an agent who can get me ten million dollars a year?' Well, let Me tell you, I'm pretty tired of it."

He was glaring at me so intently that I couldn't look directly at Him; I had to turn away. His entire being was glowing hotter than any fire I'd ever seen.

"And that's not even the worst of it," He continued. "On top of that, I get all this second-guessing! 'You shouldn't have made it rain so much, God!' 'It wasn't nice to give my son diabetes!' Oh, really? You humans know all about being nice, do you? Never a thought, even for a second, that maybe I know what I'm doing. You're all convinced that you have all the answers. Don't be so sure." With that, He spread His arms and all around me it began to grow dark.

"Sorry, God," I apologized. "But at times our lives seem so incredibly unfair."

"*Fair*? What do you know about fairness?" He roared, His very words radiating a dark light. "Let Me put it simply—I work to a different standard than you do. Maybe eventually you'll grow to the point of being able to understand, but right now, you simply don't."

With a sensation like sticking my head into a roaring lion's mouth, I said, "From what I experienced when I was alive, we certainly tried to understand, though."

God hesitated, then nodded in reluctant agreement. "Perhaps your foolish earthbound philosophers and half-witted theologians tried to explain things to you, but hardly any of them even came close." God stopped and exhaled. The dark colors faded away, and with them that awful smell.

"I'm sorry I upset You," I said to God in apology.

"Don't flatter yourself," was His reply.

Then He asked, "Jerry, did you ever read *War and Peace*? Leo Tolstoy's great novel?"

Glad to see Him calmer, I answered, "God, I'm sure You know perfectly well that I once bought a copy but couldn't get past page fourteen."

"Oh, yes, that's right, Jerry. (By the way, keep working at unlearning that awful human habit of lying about everything. It's so tiresome.) Anyway, Leo was a pretty clever guy," God said, looking more cheerful.

I blurted out, "You mean, Tolstoy had the answer? I had that book on my shelf since college, and if I'd stuck with it, I would've known the answers to life?"

God answered impatiently. "Don't be such an idiot, Jerry. And while you're unlearning, unlearn that nasty habit of interrupting. What I was going to say was that what Tolstoy understood wasn't the answers—he just had a good grip on the questions."

"Really!" I was amazed. "Is he around? Can I talk to him? Does he speak English?"

"Boy, you didn't even read the introduction to the book, did you? Leo spoke English while he was alive, for crying out loud. And yes, I wish you would keep him busy for Me if you get the chance," sighed God. "He can be such a nuisance. Just once, I wish he could finish a thought without using the word 'debauchery' two or three times. Anyway, he thinks I'm not strict enough with you people, and as I've already told you, I'm busy enough already. He ought to take a moment and think how lucky he is that I wasn't tougher on him!"

I never thought of God as being a literary critic.

"You know," He continued, "Even while I'm talking to you, one of the other things I'm doing is making the oceans boil on a little planet a couple of million light-years from your home town."

I thought of my last shrimp dinner and said, "Eeew. That sounds pretty nasty."

Whatever I was standing on started to shake. In an instant I was balanced on a pinpoint, a long, long way above where I'd been. "That's My point!" God said, wagging a gigantic fingertip up at me. "It sounds nasty to you because you're thinking of it from your infinitely ignorant perspective of cooking noodles. You don't have a clue as to what My intentions are, or what it takes for them to come to fruition."

"Actually, at the moment all I'm thinking about is not falling," I replied, feeling very unsteady.

"Don't worry about that," God corrected me. "You're in Paradise. Do you think I would let you get hurt? I'm trying to tell you something about points of view beyond your immediate concerns. That planet I was talking about is currently lifeless; what I'm doing is boiling up some chemicals so that life can get started. In about a billion years, there'll be some little creatures there. I'll let you have a look."

"That seems like a long time to wait," I answered, as I floated quickly but softly downward.

God laughed and said, "Relax. You'll still be here."

"So is that how it works?" I asked. "You set up a bunch of little factors, and let them work their way through, like a big wind-up toy?"

"Sure, sometimes," God said. "Whenever I feel like it. Other times, I take a more personal interest. Like on your grubby planet."

I felt a little offended. "Grubby? But God, with Your inspiration, of course, we've done some great things!"

God laughed and said, "Great? 'Great', you said. Creating life from rocks and gas and water—that's great. That's what I did. What did you do? Resist My will at every step; find ever more efficient ways of exploiting and brutalizing each other; destroy your own home, that puny ball flying through near-nothingness—that's what you've done."

"So why not change us?" I shot back. "Why not take all the evil within us away? You've told me that You're omnipotent, and I believe it. If You can change so much so easily, why don't You just fix everything once and for all?"

"For only one reason," God told me. "Because you—all of you—have within you not evil, but the greatness I put there—that of a little freedom and the awareness of it. It's the thing that you love most in yourselves and despise most in everything around you."

I wanted to make a protest, but He raised His hand to prevent me from speaking.

"Even though you abuse My most precious gift, I've decided to let you work that one out for yourselves." After a pause He continued. "You see? You are free to succeed or fail."

I shook my head. "But God, for many thousands of years some of us have succeeded while others have failed. I was raised that of economic necessity, some have to fail so that others can succeed."

God smiled His patient smile and softly whispered, "No, Jerry. I don't mean succeed or fail as *each* of you. I mean succeed or fail as *all* of you."

CHAPTER 9

Remembering what I could of the New Testament, I nodded and said, "Oh, I see."

"No, I still don't think you do," God said, knowing me better than I knew myself. "You retain what I think is the worst trait of humanity."

"Which is…? From talking to You, it seems as though there are so many."

God laughed and said, "I won't argue with you there! But your most dangerous quality is your monstrous ego. For as long as I can remember—and My memory goes way, way back—you have held the unshaken belief that everything on the planet exists only for you."

"Oh, I beg to differ!" I protested. "I have always shared my prosperity with others. My friends and family have all done well—and I never failed to donate quite a bit of money to charities."

"Yes," God nodded patronizingly, my clue that I had once again missed the point. "When it came to *some* other humans, you were not particularly vicious. Yet you asked Me why I don't put an end to suffering—yet what exactly had you done to end it yourself? You think harshly of Me, yet how many starving children did *you* rescue?" He held up His gentle hand and continued. "Don't bother to answer, Jerry; I already know. That boat you were so proud of, but that sat in your driveway 361 days a year—do you know how much starvation you—you, all by yourself, without direct interference from Me—could have prevented by using that money more wisely, or better still, by working to end just a little misery right around you? You see, you want to tell Me what My job should be, when you haven't held up your end of the arrangement at all. Alleviating the suffering of your fellow creatures isn't My job; it was yours."

His last words drove through my heart like a spear. In my defense, I explained that I was only doing the best I knew how to do.

His voice dropped an octave. "That's simply not true, Jerry. You knew better, but you chose not to do it. What's the real reason I don't intervene more in your lives? You—the man who complained so much about a micro-managing boss—now say that you wanted *more* intervention in your life?"

"I never thought of it that way," I confessed.

God looked directly into my eyes and said, "Of course not. Happiness, prosperity, and the eradication of misery have always been within your grasp."

"But how?"

"By simply trusting Me," He whispered. "Your sense of divisiveness about everything—what an obsolete concept! The freedom I gave you—to choose, even to believe in Me or not—what an honor, and what a disappointment to Me that so many, many, many of you second-guess Me or ignore Me or flaunt Me. If I've ever made an outright mistake (which isn't likely), it was in letting you turn your freedom into a sense of power—and want to deny freedom to others. You want to be free yourselves yet have control over the freedom of everything around you—and let Me tell you, now that it's too late to make a difference for you—that this one thing, your desire for control, has been the root of almost all of the misery that exists on your planet."

I never thought I would ever argue with God, but I insisted, "You gave us the planet and 'dominion over everything on it' if I remember my Bible…"

"That planet isn't yours, belonging to you humans!" God rumbled. "It's *Mine*—I made it, I made you, and I lent this marvelous little piece of the universe to you, to all of you, and you have gone to no great lengths to care for it. What do you think all your monuments, allegedly built to 'God's greater glory' mean to Me, when all the planet has been My cathedral? Yes, you put up some nice-looking stone mausoleums, but what was any of that compared to oak trees in the spring? Those lovely, lovely oaks that you butchered to make room for strip malls. You, Jerry, gave Me some fearful worship, but where was the simple *respect*?"

His outburst was like standing in the face of a blizzard—naked. Yet the unpleasantness simply passed through me. "God, why don't I feel ashamed? I've heard these terrible truths about me, and yet I don't feel bad."

"Of course not!" came the impatient reply. "I keep telling you, you're in Heaven, you dolt. It's exactly as I've said; it's all peace and serenity here; your soul can't be troubled, no matter how much you deserve it."

"Oh," I nodded. "I guess that's why I'm not particularly awe-struck, either."

"Yes, yes, yes," grumbled the Great One. "That's My fault, really. I give you creatures an eternity of bliss, and My thanks is that no one appreciates it. Too busy soaking up all this divine grandeur."

"It's easy to do," I informed Him, looking around.

"Of course—but up here, everything is easy for you. You'll find bliss no matter where you turn. The sad part of that is that far too many of the others who are up here are so content that they take no interest in anything."

"What do You mean?" I asked.

"It's like this—people who enjoyed running as a hobby get up here and start running and never stop, unless they get distracted somehow. That planet I told you about, where life will form after the planet has aged a billion years? By that time, hardly anyone here will take any notice of it…except Me, of course."

I wanted to say something positive. "I'm interested now, God, but I don't know how I can stay interested for that long. I can't even imagine a billion years."

God chuckled, "No, I don't suppose you can, when eight hours at your desk seemed like an eternity to you. But here, as I've told you, there really isn't any notion of time in your sense. If you want to see life forming on that planet, just close your eyes and open your mind; you will see it. Wondering how your kids, grandkids, and their off-spring are turning out? Just let it come to mind."

If it was that easy, it sounded like something that I would definitely want to try at some point. "Do many of the others up here do that?" I wondered.

"No, not really," He said.

"Why not?"

"For a reason that would be tragic if it happened under other circumstances. But you see, here not only can people have no impact on events, the events have no impact on them. Everything here is just constant, blissful bliss."

"Blissful bliss?"

"Think of when you saw your father," He said.

Remembering that, I muttered, "That really is kind of sad, in a way."

"You're right, Jerry, it would be, if you weren't in Heaven. To Me, it's more ironic than tragic. But then again, irony is one of My specialties, isn't it?"

"One of Your specialties?" I asked.

"Well, sure. The way so many things frequently work out with a subtle but meaningful little twist. Remember when you were a freshman in college, and took a train for a weekend trip to visit a friend at another school?"

"That was a long time ago," I thought.

"Then let Me help," He said.

And all of a sudden I was nineteen years old again. I was at Union Station in Chicago, sitting in a seat on a railroad coach. My small suitcase was at my feet, and I was holding a history textbook

I glanced out the window, and there was steam rising from the train next to ours. People were walking hurriedly along the platform, carrying all kinds of baggage. Late-afternoon sunlight had worked its way in through the old windows at the far end of the station. It must have been autumn, as the people I saw were wearing jackets.

Looking at myself, I saw that I was wearing a sweater instead of a jacket, and I remembered that part of my adolescent pride was that I would never admit to being cold.

The train car where I was seated was mostly empty, but filling up rapidly with many young college-age people—people my own age at that time—boarding.

I smelled dusty upholstery and burning diesel fuel.

"Oh, my, I'd forgotten all about this." Looking down at my hands, I saw that they were smooth and unscarred. My fingernails needed trimming. Suddenly I looked up as a very attractive young woman walked past and continued down the aisle.

"Do you remember this?" I heard God ask.

"It's coming back to me," I answered slowly. "I remember thinking that it would be great if some cute blonde girl sat next to me for the trip."

"And what happened next?" God's voice asked. "Do you remember that?"

This had been so long ago! But then I had a sudden flash of recollection. "That's it! A couple of minutes later, a girl—a blonde—did sit next to me!"

"The answer to your prayer, perhaps?"

I began to laugh. "Yes! Such as it was…I can laugh about it now, but it didn't seem so funny at the time. Sure enough, the girl who sat down next to me was cute, but she was only about nine years old! Her mother and brother sat in the seats directly across the aisle."

My amusement with the situation must have been contagious; God started laughing along with me. "Do you see what I mean? I really answered that prayer, didn't I? Gave you *exactly* what you asked for."

"Yes, You did," I had to agree.

"But maybe you should have been a little more specific, eh? More than a little ironic, perhaps?"

"Yes, You're right, of course. And in a way, that was when You first became real for me. There is no way on earth that could have been such a perfect coincidence." God and I were both regaining our composure.

God put His arm around me; I felt a glow like I would get from being in a hot tub after a long day of skiing. "Jerry, that's correct. There was no way…on earth…for that to have been a coincidence. You know, you're all right. That's why I decided to let you in. And I'm going to do one more thing for you. I'll show you something that I don't show just *anybody*."

CHAPTER 10

Everything around me faded to black. At last I saw a few pinpoints of light. Then more and more, until everywhere around me—above me, behind me, inside of me—there were twinkling stars, of a number higher than I would ever have time to count, even here.

"Are these all stars?" I marveled.

"Yes," God said. "But there's more. Look closer."

As my eyes became less dazzled by the light, allowing me to look around, I saw that the stars were not evenly distributed but in constellations of incredible complexity; a kind of cosmic pointillism. "What a landscape!" I cried.

"Look closer still," God suggested.

It slowly became to clear to me that each of the constellations was made up of smaller ones. These in turn broke down still smaller and smaller, until I saw only what seemed like component pieces, with a familiar pattern. "Wait a minute," I thought. "Can these really be...?"

As God began to snicker, I recognized the pattern. Each of the smallest clusters were actually cosmic dice! "See anything familiar?" He asked.

"Good Lord!" I mumbled. "That's Orion's Belt!" But from this perspective, it was just a three. I could look around it and saw a six on one side, and behind it was a four. "Is this really how galaxies are put together?" I asked God.

"Naah," He answered.. "No more so than any other representation. But you've got to admit, it is kind of a cute image, eh?" God swept up a few million dice-stars and flung them upwards. "Come on, seven! Daddy needs a new pair of shoes!" The stars spun and tumbled and whirled until they formed a spiral galaxy. God smiled gleefully, then sighed. "I just love being Me."

As I was goggling upward at the newly-formed galaxy, God turned His eyes on me and tugged at my arm. "Now let's go for a little ride."

He touched my left hand, and we were stars. Not just among stars, but actual stars, or more precisely, a galaxy of galaxies, immense in our reach. Yet we continued to change; next I became a single galaxy. From that I changed into a solar system, and continued to shrink down into a planet. The planet turned into a continent; the continent became a peninsula; the peninsula a beach. Then I was me, standing on the beach; I looked at my left hand, where God had touched me; I became the back of my own left hand. Then I was just a small patch of flesh; next a single cell; then a chromosome, a DNA molecule, an atom, a nucleus, a proton, a quark. Then as it seemed I would vanish into nothing, there was a slight pause. My thoughts were frozen as I felt a tug in the opposite direction and the entire process reversed. Once I was back to being celestially immense, there was another pause, and like a yo-yo going back and forth from the cosmic to the subatomic I changed, changed, changed. God was nowhere to be seen. Finally, with a flash I regained my original form, with God still touching my left hand. This entire experience was virtually instantaneous.

"Wow," was all I could say, and even that took a lot of effort and concentration.

"Yes, it's fun, isn't it?" God was smiling His impossibly benevolent smile.

"It certainly gave me a sense of being a part of a larger whole," I admitted.

"Maybe someday I'll let you do the entire thing, instead of just that little sample," He said.

"You mean there's more?" I couldn't imagine what it would be.

"Think for a moment," God requested. "What more might there be? Remember when you were a child, and would get on a swing…"

"You aren't going to take me back again, are you?" I interrupted.

"No, Jerry, I haven't forgotten that being on a swing used to make you nauseated, and I've got enough to keep clean as it is."

"Thank God," I said as I finally exhaled.

"You're welcome," God nodded, and continued, "Anyway, a swing is a back-and-forth cycle, and you keep going higher up and further back, until…"

"…You go all the way around! Is that what the 'whole thing' is?" I felt pretty proud of myself for figuring that one out.

"We'll see," God said, like someone who knows a lot more than he cares to reveal. "And Jerry…*please* stop interrupting, okay?"

"Okay, God."

CHAPTER 11

After my head stopped spinning, the twinkling of the stars reminded me of an army of candles I had once seen in a TV church. Recollecting that tacky spectacle made me wonder, "God, what happened to all of the televangelists? Are any of them here?"

He laughed a little and told me, "Only a very few of them made it exactly *here*, I'm sorry to say."

"Then what happened to all the other ones? Are they in some gigantic lake of fire, forced to consume burning coals, and all that?"

God said, "Ha! That would be too easy. They might learn to like it, and besides, somebody would have to be at work watching over them. So I just put them in a room someplace down a very long hallway."

"What's in the room?" I wondered.

God shrugged and said blankly, "Nothing. Nothing at all."

"That's it?" I said, astonished. "They abuse Your word, take advantage of the weak, and all they get when they die is to be put into an empty room?"

"Oh," God said, turning His face toward me. "The room isn't exactly empty. They're all in that one room, and it's not very big. Let Me assure you, none of them are happy, or ever will be. They have to put up with each other, listen to each other, and worst of all for them, argue with each other forever. And remember, that's *forever, forever.*"

"Wow, pretty nasty," I said. "I'll bet they get pretty sick of that!"

"Count on it," God said. "Every now and then they try some conspiracy or some groveling or some stupid attempt at deceiving Me, but it never works, of course. Trust Me, they're paying plenty for what they've done."

"What about their followers?" I asked, as I pictured a swarm of greasy hustlers trying to weasel their way out of each other's company.

"Oh, those people? Yes, a great many of them, to be sure. What happened to them depends on a lot of things," God told me. "Some of them are around here someplace; others aren't quite so lucky."

"So what happened to them? It seems like a lot of them were just exploited, lonely people." I felt rather sad at the thought of swarms of desolate old ladies spending eternity lost in shapelessness.

God started to explain. "You're really giving them too much credit, Jerry. You have to realize, a lot of them were definitely not very nice. They wanted things handed to them. What's far worse, a great many of them tried to bend My rules in their favor. They eagerly chased after something that they knew in their hearts wasn't right."

"Can that really be so?" I couldn't help but think of those glitzy warehouses o' Jesus packed with people, now facing eternal perdition instead of the expressway to Heaven they thought they were buying.

"There aren't many ways of straining Me," God continued. "But one of the quickest is to take My mercy for granted. People who slap a 'Christians aren't perfect, just forgiven' bumper sticker on their cars, and then presume that they have a license to behave any way they want are in for a big shock when they get to face Me in person. I'm not fooled for a minute."

I laughed a little and said, "No, I don't imagine You would be. So, do those people meet some particularly horrible fate?"

God looked straight into my eyes and gave me some serious advice. "Be careful, Jerry. You are close to enjoying the thought of someone else's misery. You're better than that."

"Sorry, God," I said humbly. "But…what does happen to them?"

"Oh, it depends," God sighed. "Often they get something ironic, like being turned into self-aware cockroaches."

"What does that mean?" I wondered.

"Well, it means that they become cockroaches, but they actually *know* that they're cockroaches when they used to be human beings. They really don't like it very much."

"Kind of like that story by Kafka?" I asked, thinking of a college literature class.

"Who?" God asked, absent-mindedly. "Oh, that guy. Well, as a matter of fact, he's one of them. Kind of gave Me the idea, to be honest."

"But don't they just run around for a while and then die, or get stepped on?" I thought.

"Nope," was God's answer. "They might get this experience for a few generations, or for a few million generations—cockroaches stopped evolving a long time ago, you know—depending on how I'm feeling at any particular moment."

"Yes, I guess that's plenty ironic," I agreed.

"One of the great things about being Me," he continued, "Is that I get to decide things in My own way. No doubt you've heard the phrase, 'God is dead'?"

It hardly seemed appropriate to admit it, but naturally I had; another of those valuable lessons from college. I didn't volunteer this information, of course.

"You may be interested to learn that Friedrich Nietzsche, who popularized that phrase, has been dwelling here ever since his death, where he gets fairly regular reminders of the inaccuracy of his idea. Serves him right, don't you think?" God asked.

"I'm sorry, God, I know I shouldn't be this way, but I can't help but laugh a little at that picture." I started a guilty chuckle.

God laughed gently along with me and said, "Oh, it's all right, Jerry. To be honest, I take kind of a wicked glee in it Myself sometimes. It's just that so many of these people were so insincere. Being that way toward each other was bad enough—but to treat Me like that? Their only sincerity was sincere selfishness. 'You can't cheat an honest man,' W.C. Fields likes to remind Me." God shook His head and grinned. "What a guy. He really keeps Me in stitches."

Half-seriously, I asked. "So, if he's here, then I guess there aren't any kids or dogs, huh?"

"Now you're just joking with Me, aren't you?" God answered. "Of course there are kids here. And so is just about every dog ever born."

This was news. I hadn't seen that many animals—or very much of anything else, for that matter. "So, there really is a doggie Heaven?"

"There's only one Heaven," God told me, matter-of-factly. "And you're in it. So are they…and cats, and spiders, and everything else. I made them all, so I had to give them a place to go, didn't I?"

I whistled and said, "This must be a big place."

"And it just keeps getting bigger."

"Sort of like the way the universe keeps expanding," I pondered.

"Something like that," He said with a nod.

"Mind if I look around some more?" I asked.

"Who am I to deny you anything?" God answered, and with that He was gone.

I started wandering around. I learned that my ideas of direction needed some adjustment. Things here are just different; terrain adapts to your movement, instead of you needing to adjust to it.

For example, even when walking uphill, there's never any strain; you just move along. Once you get used to this, you actually discover that the whole idea of up and down has no real meaning. I can't explain it; it's just something that happens. When I was a kid, I had dreams that I could run immense distances without any effort—I could move between towns, or states, or even entire countries without needing to try. Here, that kind of movement is routine.

As I explored around Heaven, I'm sure I saw lots of interesting things, and I have a vague recollection of participating in the weirdest game of bingo I'd ever experienced, but on that particular trip, nothing impressed me enough to record.

CHAPTER 12

❀

I was playing with my own imagination when I recalled something God had said.

"Hey! What do You mean, 'evolved'?" I asked of the open space around me.

The Creator appeared, wearing a lab coat. "What?"

"God, a while ago You said that cockroaches stopped evolving a long time ago."

"Yes, they did."

That seemed like a paradox. "But that doesn't seem right somehow…"

God looked a little annoyed. "Are you trying to tell Me that you've got inside news that they haven't stopped evolving?"

"Oh, sorry," I apologized. "It's just that I thought You and evolution didn't exactly…get along."

"Why not?" God answered. "What makes you think those ideas are mutually exclusive?"

"Well, forgive me for saying it…"

"You're forgiven."

"…But as I understand it, men evolved from monkeys…"

"Apes, actually, Jerry."

"Whatever. But You say You created man."

"Well, sure. I did, of course."

"Then I'm confused. How can we have evolved if we were created?"

"Jerry, for one thing, if you'd paid more attention to your science classes, you might have learned that a great many of your scientists—natural historians, especially—were also profound believers in Me."

This explanation wasn't making me feel and less confused. "How can that be? Science and religion seem like pretty separate paths," I said.

"In what way?" asked God. "If you think science is based less on faith than I am, you *really* aren't paying attention."

"I'm not sure," I answered. "If You don't mind me being rather blunt about it, science is based on proof, something that has evidence and can be done over and over with the same result. You are—how should I say it?—kind of the opposite of that."

I tensed up for a moment, hoping that I wouldn't get kicked out of here for saying that. Or get that burning toast smell again.

God dismissed my anxiety with a wave of His mighty hand. "I know what you just said seems profound to you, Jerry, but you aren't telling Me anything that I haven't heard a great many times before."

I allowed myself to exhale.

God went on, "Jerry, what people think of as solid scientific proof is pretty lame, from My perspective."

"But God," I replied, "I think there's a basic split between what can be seen and what can't."

"I'll grant you that," God said, and narrowing His glance added, "But which is more important?"

"Well, we tend to think of things that are visible as being more important," I said, being as honest as I could.

"Too bad for you," God told me. "Here, let Me give you an example. If someone showed up with lots of very visible wealth, and offered to raise one of your little girls—let's say, Jessica—should you take her up on her offer?"

"What! Of course not!"

"Why not?" God asked, looking surprised. "It's going to be hard to come up with the money to send the girls to college, and you just said that the visible is more important."

"But I love my family…and they love me! It is—okay, it was—my job to take care of them. No one can take that away from me or from any loving parent."

God smiled, "What's this talk of family love? What does that look like?"

I relaxed a little. "Oh, I see."

God patted me on the left shoulder and said, "Jerry, remember when I told you that science was an incomplete thing? Making it a little less incomplete doesn't diminish My mystery, friend. Just so you know, I *did* create you, as I created apes. That things come from other things is part of My plan, not the opposite of it. That you've chosen to catalog parts of what you've seen and tag it 'evolution' or 'natural selection' doesn't alter the underlying idea, which, to be rather forthright about it, is all Mine."

"I think I see. I guess for You that wouldn't be too hard to arrange at all." I forced a smile.

"Not in the slightest," God said confidently. "Wait till you see what I've got in store for your species, if you all can keep from killing each other long enough."

"Can I have a look?" I asked.

"Why not?" God replied. "Here, close your eyes for just a little bit and I'll give you a little preview."

I followed His instructions and held my eyes shut to allow the image to come to me. Soon I saw some figures that came into focus. Really very interesting indeed! At last I saw why humans have an appendix. Pretty clever, and not what I was expecting at all!

I opened my eyes, and was alone. I smiled, and feeling much better about one more thing, went on my way.

Wherever "my way" was leading to.

CHAPTER 13

❀

Nothing surprised me more than when I was looking around for something interesting and I saw my old friend Maggie, whose death at age 27 had been one of the major devastations of my life. My earlier talk with God about her had made me think of her often.

So at one point when I was people-watching for a while and I saw her move past, taking those energetic, purposeful steps she had had, I jumped straight up.

My sudden movement caught her attention. To my utter amazement, she recognized me instantly, and effortlessly closed the distance between us. "Jerry! I've been looking all over for you."

Sure enough, she was standing before me, her face beaming with delight.

"Maggie! It's great to see you! You look terrific." She really did, too.

"Thanks! Wow, Jerry, you're all grown up," she said, putting her arms on my shoulders. "When I last saw you, you were, what, 24?"

"Yeah, that would be about right." I couldn't stop staring at her; she never looked better.

Maggie kept smiling as she asked, "So what happened to you, Jerry?"

I looked away and answered slowly, "I'm not sure, to be honest. I think I was hit by a truck or something while I was crossing a street. Then I woke up and I was here."

She shook her head. "No, that's not what I meant. What happened to you after I came here? Did you have a good life?"

I thought for a moment and said, "You know, I believe that I did. I had a lot of fun—did some stuff that I thought might keep me out of here, to be honest—but I guess I couldn't have done too badly overall."

She tilted her head downward a little and asked softly, "Did you miss me?"

I almost felt like crying. "Of course I did. When you…died…it was the worst thing I'd ever faced. You were more alive than any two other people I'd ever met, or ever did meet." Then my voice choked off and I wasn't able to say any more.

She looked puzzled. "What's the matter, Jerry?"

Through the tears that had come to my eyes, I was able to say, "It's just that it was so unfair to lose you! You were so special…not just to me, but to so many other people. We all mourned you so much! Your poor mother…I don't know how she survived. And I know I'm not the only one who decided to live differently after you…went away."

She started to laugh softly. It hurt my feelings a little, to be honest.

"Why are you laughing?" I asked, drying my eyes. "There was nothing funny about it."

"Oh, Jerry, don't you see?" she asked, not taking her eyes off me for an instant.

"No, I guess I don't," I answered indignantly. "It was such a waste."

"A waste? No, Jerry, not at all. It wasn't a waste," she told me, her voice soothing as cool water. "When I got here, however long ago that was, God talked to me."

I brightened up. "Oh, I know, ever since I got here, He's tried to tell me what's going on around here," I said enthusiastically.

"Well…this is a little different, Jerry," she said. "God told me what I had been doing when I was alive."

"Forgive me for asking, but exactly why *were* you punished?" I asked gingerly.

"Punished?" she asked, in an amazed tone of voice. "No, Jerry, you have it all wrong. I wasn't punished, I was selected…I was given a special job. I was a teacher."

I was shocked. "A *teacher*? After seeing what happened to you, all I learned was pain."

Maggie once again put her hands on my shoulders, looked me in the eyes and said, "Now Jerry, is that really true? Didn't you just tell me that after I died, you decided to live differently? In fact, after I left, didn't you feel that life was more precious than it had been before?"

"Yes, but…" I began.

"Now, Jerry, take a moment and think about it. Be honest with yourself," she instructed.

I didn't want to think about it. "It was such a painful lesson, Maggie! You didn't have to die to teach me that!"

She stepped back and said, "Sorry, Jerry, but that's the way it works, I've learned. And once I learned that, I've always felt very honored because of it."

"So many people were so sad…" I had trouble expressing myself clearly.

"Yes, but Jerry, think of it another way," Maggie said. "How many people have you interacted with who've made no difference to you at all? In the sense that you knew it, my time was short, but I accomplished the mission God gave me…not perfectly, of course, but well enough. There is no higher honor than to improve the lives—and souls—of the people around you. And sometimes the improvements are pretty tough."

I was finally able to think for a bit; it made me feel a little better. I said to Maggie, "Yes…I'm starting to see what you mean. My world was a little larger after meeting you. And a little…deeper, perhaps."

"Now, who could ask for more than that?" she said, with obvious pleasure.

I swallowed the lump in my throat and said, "God wasn't kidding when He said that there were no easy lessons, was He?"

"Jerry, at least you learned something. Good for you!" she said. Then she began to glow. As she grew more luminous, she tapped me on the shoulder and said cheerfully, "Hey, I've got some errands to run for the Big Guy. Want to come along?"

"He makes you work?" I was astonished.

"Makes me?" she asked, in utter amazement. "Jerry, He *lets* me. Me and a few others. We get to do some pretty cool stuff. It's a big deal for us."

"You mean…you're one of the angels?" Once again, it was my turn to be amazed.

"Yes, I guess that how you'd call it," she said humbly, emitting a kind of heavenly blush.

This was simply the best news I'd gotten since arriving here. "Wow, Maggie, that's terrific! Well, it couldn't happen to a nicer person. I'm happy for you." One of my old friends was an angel. Cool.

"Listen, you want to tag along on my next errand? Really, it's okay. I've got to make an appearance in a young boy's dream. We're going to see if we can give him a subtle hint before he does something really stupid."

I wasn't aware that the angels did that sort of thing. "Hmmm…that sounds like fun, but to be honest, I'm not sure I'm ready for something like that just yet. I think I need to get my bearings around here before I can really think about going somewhere else, even for a little while. But maybe I can take a rain check?"

"Hey, no problem. Whatever you're comfortable with; that's the way it works around here. I'll see you around, okay?" she asked cheerfully.

"Maggie, you can count on it," I replied.

Once again, Maggie tapped me lightly on the shoulder, as she had habit of doing so many years ago. Then she shimmered off, as though being carried by some unseen force.

I don't think I've ever felt better.

CHAPTER 14

❀

Realizing how good I was feeling, I said out loud, "So, then, I get to stay? This isn't just a cruel joke on Satan's part?"

"Satan?" materialized God, twitching his right earlobe. "Oh, *Satan*. That's right, you probably believe in that one. He hasn't been around for ages, ever since I turned him into a third-rate Italian nobleman and sent him to dinner with the Borgia's. He was really getting to be a bore."

"What? You mean that Satan doesn't exist? But we always heard about the power of the Dark One!"

"Power? What power?" scoffed God, twitching His nose like a camel. "I'm the powerful one, for My sake. You think I couldn't just erase some paltry fallen angel?"

"But all those stories," I insisted. "There must have been something to them."

"Well, there was," said God, with a wink. "I kept him around because he had, after all, been a favorite of mine. And, he was useful for amusement—and to keep you people in line! But, then, Satan really hacked Me off one day—he invented television network prime-time programming. Bad idea, so away he went, back to medieval Italy. Funny thing is, nobody down on your little planet even noticed. You all seemed to believe he ran everything anyway, and just let it go at that. And you wonder why I don't do something about earthquakes and floods. Maybe I do."

I wondered, "How was Satan able to do something sneaky to…You?"

"I just wasn't paying attention to him that day," God replied.

I was shocked. "You weren't paying attention? But You're God; You're omnipotent; capable of anything!"

"Well, sure," God said. "I can do anything and everything, all at once. But that doesn't mean I always do."

"But why not?" I was a little offended at his inattention to detail.

He looked annoyed—or at least I think it was annoyance. His eyelids—upper and lower—were flickering like semaphores. "Maybe I just don't want to, Jerry. After all, I am God."

I was confused, after having so many ideas flung at me so quickly. "I wish I could say that I understood You better," I admitted.

"It's not that hard," was God's reply. "You just have to let go of some of your ideas about My intentions. Your confusion comes from not taking Me at face value—if you'll forgive one of My little puns."

"You see?" I said, shaking my head. "I don't have any idea what You're talking about."

"Simply this," said God. "You humans have a constant wish to interpret everything, and heap your judgments on top of My judgments. That's enough to confuse anybody."

"And yet," I answered, "We were taught 'judge not, lest ye be judged.' I tried to follow that idea."

"Not very hard, you didn't," God snapped. "You lived in a constant, unconscious sense of having superior judgment over those around you. You had no real fear of a divine Judgment Day. If you did, you would have lived differently."

I started to object.

"Don't bother," said God. "I can prove My point."

There I was, driving my good old sensible family sedan. As I passed a "35 MPH Speed Limit" sign, I looked in the rear-view mirror and saw a police car; instinctively I glanced at the speedometer. 35, on the nose. And yet my heart was racing, and I took a deep breath.

"See?" asked God, as He appeared in the passenger seat. "You are fearful of this policewoman's judgment, even though you are doing no wrong. That is how guilty your conscience is."

"I would think that it means that I lived in even greater fear of Your judgment," I replied.

"Not at all, friend Jerry. Instead, it means that you regarded My opinion as so remote as not even to be considered. And yet, what is the opinion of a cop, compared to that of the universe's Creator?" God glared at me in a way that was becoming all too familiar.

I laughed nervously and replied, "Maybe it's because I never saw a newspaper headline like *Man blasted into atoms in front of co-workers; God's wrath seen as cause.*"

God smiled a little and said, "Maybe what you saw was the end result, with a different headline."

The car dissolved and we were back to the lakeside park, home of the giant squirrel. "You truly are a most amazing God, God," I told him.

"Yes, I am," He answered, with calm confidence. "But you know, being blasted to atoms really isn't so bad," he added. Then He glanced towards me and asked, "Want to try it?"

"What! Get blasted to atoms?"

"Sure, why not?"

"I'd like to keep my current form, thank You very much," I insisted.

God looked a little pouty as He said, "Come on, Jerry, don't you trust Me?"

Finally it dawned on me. (Literally. I saw triple suns rising over some mountains in the distance that I hadn't noticed before.) I had nothing to fear. Not now. Not ever.

"You never did," God said, once again reading my thoughts. "But perhaps now you're starting to see how many possibilities are open to you once you becoming willing to rely on your faith, even when faced with what seem like impossibilities."

I couldn't disagree. "But all the same, Lord, I'll try that atom-blasting thing some other time."

"Suit yourself," He said with a sigh.

"I'm still puzzled, though. You've got the most amazing abilities; You could use them for Your benefit. You could show Your might, and make instant converts."

"Naah," God said, twitching His head. "It doesn't work like that. It's only the weakest who need to show their strength, just as it's the poorest who need to brag about their wealth."

"So what you're saying is…" I began.

"…That the strongest is also the quietest," He concluded. "Besides, if you have ever stopped to watch a hawk in flight or have seen how a tree grows from a seedling, and not believed in Me, you have already turned a blind eye to miracles greater than any of *you* will ever perform."

With that, He once again sent me on my way.

CHAPTER 15

Some time I would like to tell about all that I saw and experienced over the next while—for example, I went wandering towards an immense meteor shower and came across a rainforest full of dinosaurs!

An incredible number of them; some familiar from what I'd read about, but a great many others as well. I stopped for a moment and talked with some of the larger species. They seemed glad to have someone take an interest in them.

I wish I could tell you that they had something interesting to say, but no matter what I asked them about, they kept moving the conversation around to whether I knew where there were some tasty plants. I wanted to know what their belief in God was like, but all I got from them was some mumbling about The Fern That Feeds All, or some such thing. I eventually got frustrated with them and said to myself, "No wonder they went extinct."

I gave up on the dinosaurs and thought that humans might be better company, so I spoke with many famous people (I got to kiss Ingrid Bergman on the cheek), and a great many more who weren't at all famous, yet who had amazing stories and were endlessly fascinating. Everyone had some insight into the comparison of their mortal lives with their existence in the infinite. But all this speculation about the meaning of life, coming after I was already dead, still struck me as being very odd.

Yet in a way it was comforting to know that my religion had been the right one—after all, I was here in Heaven, wasn't I?

"Oh, Jerry, you haven't been paying attention at all, have you?" God sighed, as He appeared next to me.

"But what about those other religions?" I asked.

"What other religions?" God answered, with a furrow in His brow.

"Come on now, God, I mean like Islam or Hinduism or Shinto…doesn't my being here, and Your talking to me, mean that I was right about not following one of those false religions?"

"Don't worry so much about being *right*, Jerry. I am right. Everything else, at its very best, is only less wrong than some other thing." He shook His head and paused for a moment before continuing. "Wait…since you are so fond of stories, here's one for you."

My feet were swept out from under me and I was resting in the most comfortable recliner chair I'd ever experienced. Above my head, a scene appeared, like a movie in 3-d.

I saw a huge body of water, seemingly endless in its vastness. On this water a lifeboat floated, with forty people aboard, twenty men and twenty women.

"So here we are," someone said.

"Yes. Here we are," the others agreed.

"We need to find land," someone said.

"Yes, that would be good," came a response.

"Wait, I've found some food in a box here!" one of the people exclaimed.

Another cried out, from the other end of the boat, "And I've found some fresh water!"

"That's good," said someone else, "But we still need to find land."

"We have oars; we can row to shore!" a couple of people exclaimed.

"But which way is the shore?" another wondered aloud.

"That way is West—I can tell by the beautiful sunset," a woman offered helpfully.

"Sunset! But that means it's getting dark..." one of the people warned.

"Perhaps we'll see some land tomorrow morning," a man said. "At least it's not too cold."

"Yes, we'll be comfortable overnight, at least," the others agreed.

The scene faded to black for a while and then it began to brighten with morning. As the sun rose in the East, the people on the boat began to awaken.

"You know," one woman told the others, "I had a vision last night."

"So did I!" exclaimed another.

"Me, too!" said a third.

Soon it became evident that every single person on board the boat had had a vision the night before. (Actually, only five of them had, but nobody wanted to be left out, so they agreed with the others.)

One man stood up and said, "Last night, an Angel of the Lord appeared to me and said, 'Row West, young man, row West!'"

"That's odd," said a woman. "Last night, *two* Angels of the Lord appeared to me and said, 'Salvation lies to the North!'"

Not to be outdone, a third person claimed, "In my vision, Saint Paul appeared to me and said, 'In the South shalt thou find thy safe harbor.'"

The fourth prophet insisted, "Jesus Christ *Himself* appeared to me last night and proclaimed simply, 'Hosanna! Eastward.'"

Finally, a woman stood in the center of the boat and solemnly pronounced, "The Almighty appeared to me and said, 'Humble, pious Lady, remain calm and I shall rescue those who truly believe in Me. Until then, I shall provide.'"

Needless to say, what followed was a lot of confused talk. By the end of that day, the people aboard the lifeboat discovered that there were five distinct groups, each with eight members. Each group remained adamant, and a continually renewed argument lasted long after darkness fell, until everyone was so exhausted that they collapsed, and did not awaken the next day until long after sunrise.

"Well, here we still are," said Prophet One. "Stuck because the rest of you haven't seen the right answer."

"On the contrary," replied Prophet Five. "We have stayed still, as our Lord has asked."

"A great way to starve," volunteered Prophet Three.

"My people will wait no longer," insisted Prophet Four, and her group took their oars and began to row to the North.

"Wait a minute," said Prophet Two, and his group began to row to the East.

Realizing that their sense of correctness was at stake, two other groups also grabbed oars and began rowing in their chosen direction. During all this, the fifth group looked smugly around them at the foolishness of the others.

After a day's worth of furious splashing about, the boat had not moved. So darkness fell upon them for the third time. Taking no chances, each group appointed the two least-exhausted believers to keep watch on the others to make sure no one cheated and rowed while the others were asleep.

During a quiet moment, one of the Easters whispered to one of the Northers. "Hey, pal."

"What do you want, heretic?" came the reply.

Patiently, the Easter said, "We don't need to argue. Let's just cooperate, and we can overcome the others by just rowing to the Northeast!"

"What's in it for us?" the Norther asked.

The Easter told him, "Closer is better than farther. Besides, I've heard that the Westers are planning to kill us all."

"Why, those dirty…" there was evident anger in the Norther's voice. "But shouldn't we warn the Southers?"

"My friend, our work is cut out for us. We'll strike first. The Westers will be taken care of, and the Southers will toe the line. We'll need them to help do the rowing. Right?"

The Norther nodded. "I...I guess so."

"Good," said the Easter. "Tell your people—quietly!—and I'll tell mine, and we'll strike just before dawn."

And so it happened; just as there was enough light to see, the Westers were completely surprised—because after all, there had been no plot—had their throats cut, and were dumped overboard. A blood-red sunrise revealed twenty-four remaining people in the boat.

"Hey," said the Norther Prophet. "What happened to the Prayer Group?"

"They were a waste of space," said the Easter prophet. "As non-true believers, they were merely taking up food and water that the rest of us will need on our journey to the North...Northeast, I mean."

"Outrage!" claimed one of the Southers. "How dare you slaughter the innocent? We would rather die than assist you—in fact, we will purge your kind from this world!"

Another melee ensued, with the exhausted Easters and Northers fending off the rage of the Southers. Given a taste for blood, the Northers and Easters did eventually overcome and kill all the Southers, but in so doing each group lost four of its members. So by sundown on the fourth day, there were only eight remaining people in the boat. Overwhelming fatigue left them unable to move, while the boat remained in place for another night, surrounded by floating corpses.

The morning of the fifth day finally saw some movement, in a Northeasterly and then Eastnortherly direction. "Now we're getting somewhere," they all agreed.

But before much longer came a cry. "Wait a minute!" accused one of the Easters of one of the Northers. "You're cheating toward the North!"

"I am not—you are cheating toward the East, and I'm just compensating," came the retort.

"But East is the True Way! Heading North will only invoke the wrath of God!"

"Blasphemous dog! What do you know of truth? North is the path to land! East is the land of the unholy!"

Another fight—four more dead bodies fed to the fishes. Now only two Northers and two Easters remained. They moved to opposite ends of the boat.

"At least we have the water supply," said one Norther to the other.

"Glory to God, we have the food!" rejoiced one Easter to her companion.

After watching the Easters eat their evening meal, one of the Northers began laughing. "What's so funny, Norther devil?" cried one of the Easters.

"You fools! I poisoned that food!" the Norther replied, scarcely able to contain herself.

That night the two remaining Easters died of horrible convulsions. The next morning one Norther said to the other, "So, what are we supposed to eat, now that you've poisoned the food?"

"Don't you see?" her comrade replied. "You and I, we're like Adam and Eve. All we have to do now is row North, to where the land is."

But they never made it. The boat was simply too large to be rowed by two weakened people. In fact, all the struggling on board had put some small leaks in the boat, and the two were barely able to bail fast enough to keep the boat from sinking. Though they had plenty of water, the two died of exhaustion two days later, just as the sun set.

The darkened image turned into vapor, and I was once again standing.

I didn't get it. "So which way was the land?" I asked God.

He sighed and said, "Not that it really matters, Jerry, but there was land all around them. All they had to do was move in any direction—but work together to do so."

"But how could they cooperate with their enemies?" I wondered.

God said, "Their enemies? There were no enemies in that boat, Jerry. The enemy was around them, not among them. Don't you see, Jerry, that by insisting on being right, and wanting to punish those who disagreed, all they accomplished was their own self-destruction?"

"But they had such different visions, God," I said.

"Really? Were they so very different?" God asked.

There was a dramatic flash and God was gone. He left me with an oar in my hands.

CHAPTER 16

❀

When the smoke cleared I said, "That's very clever, God, but I still have to wonder about something."

God materialized behind me and said, "Yep…You want to know why it is that the early religions on your planet worshipped animals, or the sun, or astrology, or some thing other than Me before the idea of Me came into being."

"Yes, exactly! Thanks for putting it so clearly."

"No problem. It's back to the idea of learning. I can't reveal more to you than you can accept at any time. Your kind needed to grow up a bit before I could really extend the idea of My being out to you."

"You mean the way we're taught in school simple physics before we get to understanding molecular structure and subatomic particles."

"Very good, Jerry! Can you explain what a quark is?"

"Well, no, I can't, God. Wasn't one of our first conversations about my bad science skills? But I seem to remember that quarks were important for some reason or other. Aren't they?"

"I can never remember either. Anyway, your inability to understand things doesn't mean that they don't exist, or aren't important, does it?"

"Of course not. If the whole world was only as smart as me, it wouldn't be a terribly smart place, I guess...though it's a little embarrassing to admit it," I said, blushing to myself.

God gave me His reassuring look and said, "Okay. I'm not going to argue with that. Now think about this. Does your inability to understand something at a given moment mean that you'll never understand? Or might it not also mean that one day you will understand it?"

I thought for a bit and said, "I guess that's why religions have evolved, too. They started out primitive and explained You in more sophisticated ways as we were able to understand You a little better."

"Yes, that's close, but you're about to make a big mistake..." God warned.

"So my religion, which emerged from others, must be better!" I felt pretty proud of myself for figuring that one out. I folded my arms confidently.

"Oh, Jerry, once again, you've missed the point," The Almighty sighed.

"Hold on, God," I bristled. "You just told me..."

"Jerry, what I told you was in a grander sense of humanity, not your petty hair-splitting interpretations of My meaning."

"What?" Once again, He had left me behind.

God took a deep breath and exhaled half of it before explaining. "Okay, Jerry, let's try it your way. You're right. The ideas I've planted as an essential part of your being...those ideas that first found expression in worship of nature, then the goddess—a somewhat better idea, relatively speaking. Next you moved on to the whole catalog of what were called gods; a different spirit for each part of nature—both yours and Mine. So far, so good."

God let that sink in before continuing. "Once you started to think of Me in this form, you were getting warmer still. But that took a lot of work, and time. Now, though, you're telling Me that you've figured out how to speed up the process! You think that one particular interpretation of Me, written long ago, and translated over the years from language to language, and interpreted by men, and re-interpreted by other men, and adjusted from generation to generation, and split by schism and warfare, adapted to local cultures, reworded and debated and fought over...after all this, somehow, by some pure accident, *you* (of all people) are now in the sole possession of the absolutely correct version of what I'm all about?"

"Ummm..." was the only defense I could muster.

"Exactly," God said. "What direction did *you* row in, Jerry?"

And He disappeared in a huff of smoke.

CHAPTER 17

❀

God's words echoed in my ears for quite a while. After turning them over in my mind for the hundredth time, I shook my head. I sat down on a nearby chair and muttered into empty space, "I guess we just face so many choices. It's hard to know what to do. I can remember really wanting to have the answers."

Suddenly God was standing next to me—but He was standing on His head. "Yes," God nodded in agreement, as He rotated into a more conventional pose. "It's not easy to find the right balance between faith and awareness. The way I see it is that what you really need isn't answers, but a better way to understand the questions."

"You mean," I responded, "That if we don't understand a question completely, we can only give incomplete answers at best, or more likely, answers that are simply wrong?"

"Jerry, you amaze me!" God beamed. (And when God beams, He really *beams*.) "You're finally starting to catch on."

"If I learned one thing while I was alive," I said, "It's that easy answers are so few and far between. I sure didn't get much from the self-help books I read."

"Not surprising, is it?" God asked. "Now that you realize how complicated everything is, you can see how superficial the peddlers of quick solutions are."

I recalled the last such book I'd read, about the differences between men and women, and how I thought at the time that a better understanding of women might improve my marriage.

God nodded, sharing my recollection. "Let Me begin by telling you that your motives were good, Jerry. But how did you expect to have a better marriage by reading something written by someone you've never met?"

"That's not what I was expecting from the book," I clarified. "I just never have understood women very well, not even my own mother."

"Oh, Jerry," God said, "Even reading a book about toasters wouldn't help you fix the one you've got. Each one is different, and has to be treated differently."

"Still, there seem to be some general similarities among women," I observed.

"There are superficial similarities among many, many things," God said. "And yet each is unique. When a flock of sparrows is startled, some fly off one way, some another, still others don't move at all. Could you point to one in particular and predict what she's going to do? And don't I even plan all snowflakes to be just a little different? Think about how much more complex your wife is compared to a snowflake or a sparrow, and then tell Me exactly how you could expect this book to help."

"Yes," I admitted, as my thoughts drifted. Why did I prefer Sarah over the other women I had met? Why had she chosen me, for that matter? And now that I was gone, would she remarry?

"Good questions," God responded. "If all men and women were alike, why would it matter whom you chose? Why divorce and remarry if it makes no more difference than eating at two different outlets of the same fast-food chain?"

"Because it does matter," I said.

"Your darn tootin'," said God with a wink. "Be glad of it."

Like all humans, I had my insecurities, and although I knew they no longer amounted to anything, I couldn't help but wonder if my marriage had been more or less happy than other people's.

"You actually did pretty well," God said. "In My opinion, you made some good choices in your marriage. And My opinion counts for a lot."

"So tell me, then," I asked. "What was it that I did so well? At the time, it seemed like a lot of work."

God tapped me on the left shoulder, in just the way Maggie had done. "Exactly! Marriage is like most other things in life; it isn't what you get out of it that matters—it's what you put into it."

I felt a little better. "So, do You think we humans should make divorce harder to obtain?"

"No, I think you'd be far better off if you made *marriage* harder to obtain. Too many people put as much thought into choosing a mate as they put into buying a new coat, so they get each about as frequently." God shook His head solemnly. "I'll say it again—I wish you'd pay more attention to what I have to teach."

CHAPTER 18

❁

"But God, I was told that You sent Your one and only son to Earth to teach us…and give us everlasting life."

God explained, "Yes, Jerry, that's another thing that a lot of you talk about when you first get here."

"Well, then, doesn't that mean that Jesus Christ really was divine?"

I was shocked at His answer. "I don't really remember," He said.

I sputtered like a moped. "What! You don't remember! How can that be?"

"Calm down, Jerry. Let Me ask you a question. Remember when you closed on your house?"

"Yes—it was a very big day for the whole family. I—we—were very nervous about it."

"You signed a lot of papers that day, didn't you?"

I laughed and said, "You bet. Deeds, loan certificates, titles—and checks! There were enough documents there to paper a large room."

God nodded as He remembered along with me. Then He gently asked, "Now tell Me—what kind of pen did you use?"

"Excuse me?" That was not the question I was expecting.

God persisted. "Come on! What kind of pen was it? Goose-quill? Bic? Parker? Quick, it's important! Shaeffer? Papermate? Mont Blanc? Fine point? Medium? Felt-tip? Tell Me right now!"

At first I was confused by the rapid questions, but then I just smiled. "Umm…God, I don't remember because it wasn't the pen that was important. It was my sign of commitment that made the difference."

God glared and said, "Exactly. All those silly questions—'Where exactly was the Garden of Gesthemane?' 'Did Christ really look like a hippie?' 'What did they serve for appetizers at the last supper?' What difference does it make? Talk about not seeing the forest for the trees!"

But I couldn't give up that easily. "I'm sure that's true, Lord, but I do know one thing for sure—when I signed the really important stuff in life, I didn't use a pencil."

God had inhaled, ready to go on talking, until He heard my statement. Then He stopped in mid-breath and turned toward me. Then, to my utter astonishment, He laughed quietly. After a moment, He said, very softly, "Jerry, you're a wise man."

That certainly took me by surprise. I wasn't sure what He meant. "Wise in what way, God?"

He smiled and said, "Deep down inside you, there's a germ of real faith. I like that. I think that's why you're here. Somehow you always knew what was right and what was wrong."

"Is that unusual?" I wondered to myself.

"No," God said in response to my private thought, "What's unusual is that every now and then, you paid attention to it."

"Thanks," I said, without being really sure what I was thanking Him for.

"If only more of you could pay attention to that voice, and learn to ignore all that other meaningless stuff," He said wistfully. "Can it really matter where some historical event took place, when My very meaning is something that is beyond what you know as time and space?"

I didn't know if He was being rhetorical or not, so I said, "We put an awful lot of time and effort into worrying about that sort of thing, God."

He nodded in agreement. "I know. But any time spent worrying about it is too much. Why not just accept the message? It is a good one; one of My very favorites. If you saw 'Love Your Neighbor' spray-painted on a mural, wouldn't it still be a great idea? It's a sure sign of small-mindedness to focus on the trivia and miss the whole point."

Despite God's recent compliment, I felt compelled to defend my species. "To me, I always thought we were just trying to do our best," I said.

God waved one of His mighty fingers and corrected me once more, an experience I still hadn't learned to like. "No, far too often you used Me simply as an excuse to do what you wanted. When I think of all the prayers I've heard that start with, 'Kill my enemy, in Thy glory,' I sometimes want to obliterate you all and start over."

"So why don't you?" I asked.

For the briefest of instants, anger flashed on God's face.

Then He looked directly and intensely into my eyes, and I could see what He was picturing to Himself.

In a large meadow, the sun was shining on a young girl, no more than three years old. She wore a light blue dress with a bunny rabbit embroidered on the front. As I focused my attention on her, she knelt down to get a close look at a dandelion, her dark brown hair falling forward and covering the sides of her face. Just as her button nose got within a few inches of the blossom, a honeybee, oblivious to the girl, landed on the flower. Rather than being afraid, the girl sprang up in delight and spun around to attract the attention of her mother, who was standing close by. The most important thing in the world was the little girl's desire to share with her mother her discovery of a honeybee.

As God spoke, the scene faded from His eye.

"I see this many, many times," God whispered, and I would have sworn He had a small tear in His eye. "I don't think I could continue to exist without it. You know that saying, 'God is love'? Well, it's true, truer than you can ever know. If I, of all beings, withhold My love, I believe that I would cease to exist."

This was a side of Him that I hadn't seen before. "I guess You do love all Your children," I said. "Or is that another of my many misunderstandings?"

"No, that part is correct," God patiently informed me. "I do love you all. Unconditionally. But that doesn't mean I don't get angry. Now if you'll excuse Me, I'd like to be alone."

Where God had been standing I saw a huge panoramic landscape painting of incredible liquid luminosity. Then the image became real, or at least real to me.

CHAPTER 19

One of the oddest things about Heaven is that it seems empty whenever I want it to be, and yet things and people and activity are as close as my whims. It's a whole universe of take-it-or-leave-it, with every result being pretty much the same.

Just as God had told me earlier, after my first encounter with my Dad, all the pretenses of life were now gone. That changed a lot of behaviors, but it didn't bother anybody. After a while, it didn't even bother me, for the most part. There was a very refreshing quality to the honesty and forthrightness of the people I met here (few though they were).

I couldn't help but compare that to the kind of social problems I remembered from being alive. In all of my social interactions, there was a constant awareness and sensitivity to others' feelings...except when driving, of course. The contrast was so stark that I felt that it would be a good thing to ask God about.

Sure enough, as soon as that thought formed in my head, there He was. On this occasion, He was wearing what looked like judicial robes.

"I didn't interrupt anything important, did I?" I asked as politely as I could.

"Not possible," was all He said in reply. "Now, tell Me what's on your mind."

We chatted for a while about human organizations, and why they are the way that they are. As we talked, I came to realize how very frail social structures are.

"The level of conflict in your societies never fails to amaze Me," God told me at one point.

I was reluctant to bring it up, but finally I said, "Well, Lord, it always seemed to me that many of our conflicts have been the result of disagreements about one topic."

God slowly raised one eyebrow and asked, "What topic would that be?"

"You," I said.

"Ah, yes," He nodded in agreement. "Such a pity."

I shook my head and said, "I guess we haven't been very successful at loving our neighbors."

"That may have an element of truth, but that's not the biggest part of the problem as I see it," God said. In response to my puzzled look, He said, "After all, you were told to love your neighbors as yourselves."

"And?" I asked.

"Well, the sad reality is that that's about what you do. The real issue is that you just don't love yourselves very much. If you did, you might see your world in a clearer light."

"I don't get it," I had to admit. "You've been telling me how egotistical and selfish we are, but now You say we don't love ourselves enough? That seems like a real Catch-22."

"Nothing of the sort!" rumbled God. "Where did you get the idea that selfishness and vanity have anything to do with love? Think in terms of respect and sincerity and nurturing. Those are the fields where real love grows." After a moment, He concluded by saying, "Love is about wanting the *best* for something, not the *most*. Love doesn't mean buying your wife a bigger TV, it means turning the stupid thing off and having an intelligent conversation."

"To my own family, I just wanted to be a good provider," I admitted. "Sometimes it got pretty competitive."

God reassured me, "Jerry, you were a good provider. Your fault was not knowing when you'd provided enough. Hardly anyone does. Your culture worships wealth, but isn't unique in that regard. Yet if you stop and think, did you ever meet a rich person you'd trade places with?"

I thought for a moment and answered, "Now that I think about it, no. My wealthy friends—not that I had very many—seemed to spend all their time worrying about keeping their money, trying to get more, all the time convinced that everyone only liked them for their bank balances."

God raised His eyebrows and said, "You were a little like that yourself, weren't you?"

I had to laugh at my past self. "Yes. Does that mean that I had too much money?"

"I think you've already answered that," was all God would say.

I felt a little defensive, and managed to say, "Nobody's perfect, God."

"Except Me, of course. Fear not, Jerry, I'm not holding you personally responsible. If you ever provoke My wrath, you'll know it." With that, He chuckled a bit and shrank into a size that made Him invisible to me—or had I just inflated myself so much that I could no longer see Him?

CHAPTER 20

❀

That last remark of His struck me as curious. This is Heaven, I thought. It's paradise, an unending ocean of divine splendor. Was it even possible to provoke God in His own back yard?

"Sure it is," He told me, appearing once more. "Every now and then, a bug crawls onto the cake, so to speak. And it becomes necessary for Me to take care of it."

"But how?" I asked. "This is the state of eternal divine grace, isn't it?"

"In the sense that it's a dwelling of infinite bliss and peace, yes. But there is this curious habit some people have of trying to poison the well. They do it very insidiously…"

"They try and betray You?" I guessed.

God scowled, and my teeth started to rattle. "No, Jerry, they interrupt me once too often, and I condemn them and all their families to eternal perdition! Who could anyone possibly betray Me to? Now be quiet and let Me finish."

After my mouth came to rest, God continued. "Their crime is to leave behind offspring who have the potential to do better, or at least get no worse, but these children revel in misery. They discover an appetite for evil that they can only satisfy through corruption."

Waiting until I was sure it was safe to comment, I said, "I've known people like that. But are you saying that they're under the influence of their heavenly ancestors?"

God nodded His eyebrows. "Indirectly. While alive, their predecessors had the chance to make the world a better place, *even through their evil actions*. But if they left behind too many seeds of greater evil, they don't stay here long. I send them away."

"Where do they go?"

"You don't want to know," God said flatly.

"But God," I protested, "You know how curious I am. Are You telling me there really is…a hell? Lake of fire and all?"

God sighed one of his enormous breaths and said, "Actually, Jerry, it's a great deal worse than that. Those who leave here just go elsewhere…but it isn't here. They are just somewhere else. It doesn't matter where. But having had a taste of Heaven, they are forever tormented by what they have lost."

"I'm not sure I understand."

"Don't you see? It's the most horrible punishment I could subject them to. It removes all doubt—and all hope. They aren't tormented by demons, or subject to physical deprivations. But their souls are broken."

As I began to understand the meaning of His words, I could only shake my head and say, "Forgive me for saying this, God, but it seems rather cruel."

He snorted and said, "Never mind about passing judgment on Me. We've been over that. But before you get too comfortable around here, perhaps you should take a moment and start thinking about what seeds you planted while you were alive."

CHAPTER 21

Thinking about that actually made me feel tired; this was the first time a sensation of exhaustion had happened since my arrival. It felt kind of odd; although I had had episodes of confusion, I had gotten so used to feeling alert that it took me a while to remember what it was like to want to lie down and actually fall asleep.

I figured that there wasn't much point in worrying about finding a comfortable place, so I decided to have some fun with the idea of taking a nap. I started running; faster and faster, in no particular direction. Then I leapt upward, and continued to accelerate. Although I was still a little uneasy with the sensation of flying, I decided to let go of my fears, and I closed my eyes and fell asleep, even as I flew onward.

God appeared to me in a dream. "Learning to like it here at last, Jerry?"

"I think I am finally getting over my anxieties about everything. I trust You...but what are You doing now?" I asked, as I noticed His hands moving rapidly.

God smirked at me and said, "Just a little juggling. Here, have a look."

In His hands I saw a number of objects that He was juggling in a circle. After watching a few cycles, I noticed that God was juggling an eyeball (yecch), a sweet potato, a tied piece of rope, a conch, an iceberg (a *big* one), and some kind of fish.

He really had me this time. "Do you get it, Jerry?"

"Not really," I had to admit. "Though You could probably get a couple of weeks in Vegas being able to keep all that stuff in the air."

God gave me His stop-being-so-silly look. "Oh, Jerry, don't you know Me better than that by now? Here, it's a little puzzle. I'll explain it to you."

And so he slowed down the movement of the objects, and explained the first one as he caught and then tossed it. "Eye." Then the second item. "Yam." Along came the length of rope. "Knot." The next, "A shell." Then, "Ice." And finally, "Cod."

"You're too mysterious for me, God," I said as I shook my head.

"Keep watching, Jerry. Eye...yam...knot...a shell...ice...cod. Now, repeat after Me."

Odd though it was, it would be unwise to turn down this kind of offer. "Eye-yam-knot-a shell-ice-cod."

"Okay," God said. "Keep going."

Finally, it came to me. "Oh! 'I am not a jealous god!' Really?"

"Really." God nodded slowly as He spoke. "One question I get a lot is, 'Are there people from all religions in Heaven?' Of course there are. However individuals define Me, their sincere reverence gains them access. Perhaps to their own minds they have 'attained enlightenment'; I don't much care. Here, they can believe whatever they want to believe—which is pretty much how you humans live anyway."

"We do have so many fragmented religions," I agreed. "Like what we talked about earlier, all the different types of churches."

God growled, "When I say that I am not a jealous god, I mean that I *know* I am the ultimate. You may choose to *believe* it or not, but your lack of faith in Me, while a little distressing, in no way detracts from Me or My power. It's not the number of churches that concerns Me. It's the things that you are all actually worshipping."

"Like what?"

"*Things*, I said," God repeated. "You forsake worshipping the eternal in exchange for the worship of the transitory. That's a bad idea, and a bad bargain. When you were on earth, all around you was only temporary, not to mention you yourself. What is there left to worship, or even admire, when that all goes away? Because this you can believe: All possessions, all pleasures, all people will fade into dust, and then even the dust will fade. I am all that endures. Love Me, do not fear Me, and I will joyously share eternity with you."

I was certainly enjoying eternity so far. I said, "But it seemed like You were so demanding. The Ten Commandments…"

God nodded and told me, "The Commandments; do I actually expect you to follow them to the letter? It's safe for Me to tell you that to be perfectly honest, no. They are a little extreme. For example, do I really expect you not to kill? Hardly; even a vegetarian has to kill plants in order to eat. But if you kill anything wantonly—your fellow men, My creatures, or especially forests, you offend Me."

"Then what's the point?" I asked.

God said, "The Commandments give you something to strive toward, do they not?"

"Sure," I answered, "But they seem so unattainable."

"Well, they may have a certain strictness to them, but that's for your own good. Let's take one example. What good does it do you to covet?"

"God, if you're waiting for me to argue with you about this one, I'm going to disappoint you. I tried really hard not to covet my neighbors'…things," I told Him.

"If that's what you want to believe, fair enough," He replied, giving me that knowing look of His. Then He asked, "But are you sure you wouldn't like to have one of *these*?"

In His hand there appeared a large diamond. It was huge, blue-white, a perfectly cut trillian. But more than that, it was alive. It didn't just look alive; I could tell it was a living thing. It beckoned to me, giving me the distinct impression that it wanted me to take it from God's hand.

I felt a longing for it that was more intense than anything I could ever remember. The living diamond had some sort of power over me; the aching in my heart was far, far worse than the bittersweet yearning for my first love.

"Oh, Jerry…" God said, shaking His head in disapproval.

I was unable to stop myself from asking, "Please…may I have it?" I couldn't take my eyes off the diamond.

"So, what would you give up to have this?" It was unlike God to offer to bargain.

My need for the diamond was choking me; I could hardly breathe. "I…guess I don't have anything to offer anything in exchange," I managed to say. "But maybe You could make a gift of it to me?"

"Why should I do that?" God asked.

"Well…you're God," I argued. "You could easily make another one."

"I already have," He informed me. "Want to know how to get one?"

"Of course I do," I snapped. "Why are You tormenting me like this?"

Instead of getting angry with me, He simply asked, "Jerry, haven't you figured this one out yet? Why have I ever done anything to you?"

I closed my eyes. Slowly I came to the realization that this had to be one of His lessons. I reached into the pocket of the pants that up till then I hadn't realized I was wearing, and pulled out a living diamond of my own.

"See? It was there all along," said The Almighty.

"Somehow I knew there would be one there," I said, unable to take my eyes off the glimmering, pulsating jewel. "I guess it's one of those things I didn't know I had."

"Kind of makes you stop and think, doesn't it?" God asked.

I nodded. "Yes. I can't help but wonder how much of my life was populated with precious things I didn't know about."

"You can say that again," God answered. "You see, there's so much more to coveting than simple materialistic envy. Covetousness isn't just bad for the thing being coveted; it's worse for you. It takes possession of you and controls you and will eventually destroy you. Worst of all, it causes you to discount the real value of your life. No *thing* is worth that."

"You had me going for a while," I confessed, unable to repress a self-conscious smile.

God smiled back as He answered. "You'd be surprised how many people take forever to catch on to that one, Jerry. You did well by not obsessing…not too much, anyway. I knew My trust in you wasn't misplaced."

Another compliment! He'd be spoiling me if this kept up. "So, okay, God, we're in agreement on that Commandment. But that's one in ten. How could anyone possibly keep up with all of the rest of them?"

"Jerry, instead of My answering that directly—you know how I dislike doing that anyway—let Me ask you a question. If you believe the Commandments to be so imperfect, so restrictive, so burdensome, how else would you have it?" God asked. "Imagine, if you can, a world in which the opposites of these Commandments are revered. Death, destruction, discord, anarchy; or perhaps worst of all, a universal apathy. Your culture totters on the brink of this daily, and has for thousands of years. That is the burden you place upon yourselves by not listening to Me. Many of you declare the Commandments unreachable, and resign yourselves to an existence of crawling in filth, without ever bothering to look up, or even look around. What sort of world—and what kind of heaven—do such people deserve?"

With that, I awoke from my dream. I was still flying, and I noticed that I was about to slam into a mountaintop. After an anxious instant, I remembered from my previous experience with heavenly flying that I should probably just float through anything, so I was a bit shocked when I hit the mountain with full force and stopped. It didn't hurt…but I found that I had a lot of little pieces of granite in my teeth.

Slowly I slid down to the base of the mountain. I shook the loose dirt and rocks from out of my hair, but try as I might, I couldn't quite get all the little pieces of granite from my teeth. I really needed some serious flossing, but none was around. The sensation was very unpleasant, and becoming ever more irksome.

Finally, in frustration I looked around for someone to help me—I just couldn't bring myself to ask for God to help me clean my teeth! A few people were drifting nearby. I waved to the nearest one, a blond woman.

"Excuse me," I began, "I…"

She stopped for a moment and looked at me. In an emotionless voice she said, "You've already been excused, or you wouldn't be here." She then continued on her way.

I said, "No, wait, I just wanted to ask you a question."

She stopped walking and gave me her full attention. "If you're going to ask me a question, then you should know that my name is Olga," she informed me. "What's your name?"

"Hello, Olga, my name is Jerry." I extended my hand in greeting.

"I don't like being touched," she said.

"Oh…I'm sorry," I answered, feeling more than a little embarrassed. I stuck my hands in my pockets before going on. "But I've got something stuck in my teeth…"

Bristling with indignance, she snapped, "Don't expect me to clean your teeth for you. Who do you think you are?"

Barely able to overcome my shock, I tried to defend myself. "Well, all I wanted to know is where I could get some help…I wasn't really expecting you to actually do the cleaning."

"Why not?" she answered. "Aren't I good enough?"

"But you just said…"

She put her hands on her hips and lectured me. "Look, it's like this. If you want something done for you, just go around the nearest corner and it'll be there. Dental work, shoe repair, gourmet food, neighborhood pub, angioplasty, you name it. Don't you know anything?"

The cleverest thing I could think of saying was, "I've only been here a short while, and I…"

Olga interrupted by saying, "Well, who's been showing you around? Give me his name, and I'll remind him of what he's supposed to be doing."

I thought for a second and said, "Are you sure you want His name? I mean, I don't want to get anyone in trouble."

"Are you kidding?" Olga said with massive indignance. "It's everyone's responsibility to see that we keep the right standards around here, or the place will just go all to…well, you know what I mean."

I sighed. "Okay…but my tour guide since I got here has been God."

I expected her to be impressed.

"Yeah, right," she shot back.

"No, really," I insisted, leaning into her a little. "He's been telling me about all kinds of things since I got here."

Looking as skeptical as a teenage girl being approached by a predatory salesman, she said, "Now, why in Heaven's name would God waste His efforts on *you*? Have you got any idea how many people are here, and how busy God is just keeping things going? I've been here ever since I can remember, and I've never even *met* God."

"I don't know about all that," I told her. "All I know is that ever since I got here, He's been very nice to me, telling me all sorts of things."

With a snicker, she said, "Oh, Jerry, I think someone's been pulling your leg. That 'Welcome to Heaven, I'm God' gag is as old as death. You probably just got hooked up with some egotistical blowhard who decided to impress you by giving you his idea of how things should be."

That was a statement I wasn't prepared for at all. My shoulders sagged and I sat down.

She wasn't finished. "Do you mind if I ask you something, Jerry. Did he do the old living diamond trick?"

My jaw dropped. "How did you know?" I asked.

Shaking her head, Olga said, "I can't believe how many of you fall for that one. Just like small children, only dumber."

Where had I heard that before?

She went on. "Look, friend, if you're going to make it here, you're going to have to learn not to be such a dope."

I started to feel confused and very shaky.

Olga brought me out of my reverie by saying, "Look, before you do anything else, please go get those teeth fixed, okay? It looks really gross. What did you do, fly into a mountain or something? Now I've got to be going. Nice talking to you."

And with that, she trotted off, before I had the chance to say another word.

To say that I was stunned doesn't begin to describe it. Could it really be true? The character that I had accepted as God, just another lifeless entity, no different from me—only perhaps a lot more eloquent? The irritation of the rocks in my teeth was nothing compared to the jagged boulders that I felt growing inside me.

It seemed as though everything around me was just an illusion; that the clouds beneath me were just watercolor paintings that would dissolve and vanish into nothing…and I would vanish right along with them.

CHAPTER 22

❀

I don't remember how long I stayed like that. Everything that I had been getting used to; all of my sense of comfort and belonging seemed to be false. It was difficult enough to be in a place without time and place—to be without a moral direction was far worse.

Vaguely I remember seeing others, and wanting only to avoid them, for fear that they, too, would give me some revelation that would confuse me even further.

I think my greatest anxiety was that here, where I expected to spend the rest of eternity, would never be a place in which I could really be comfortable, as though all the doubts and fears that I had had when alive would persist forever, in a way that no amount of ice cream sundaes or hypnotic illusions could dispel.

My overwhelming sense was that of being lost. Literally a lost soul, I thought to myself. Some Heaven.

With nothing better to do, I retraced my experiences since arriving here. I remembered the meeting with my father, and how vague he seemed; had he really been an illusion?

Had those discussions with "God" been nothing more than an indication of my own willingness to be taken in by someone who merely seemed like an authority figure?

At last I realized that there was only one way to find out.

"God," I spoke.

"Yes, Jerry?" came His patient reply. "Something is troubling you, I see."

"I guess You know what it is," I said hopefully, hoping that God's omniscience would be of some help to me.

"Of course I do, but I think you'd feel better if you'd just tell Me," He suggested.

Maybe He really doesn't know! I thought. God just looked at me and smiled His patient smile.

I stood silent for a bit and unable to think of any other way to phrase the question, blurted out, "God, how do I know You're You? How do I know that even here in Heaven, You aren't an impostor?"

God gave me a very puzzled look for a moment, studying me very intensely. Then He said, in a very serious tone of voice, "Jerry, you've got something in your teeth."

"What?" was all I could manage to say.

Without a change of expression, He explained, "You look like you've got little pieces of something in your teeth. Would you like Me to take care of that?"

I had forgotten all about the leftover rocks. "Sure," I answered. Then, a little nervous about how exactly to proceed, I asked, "Do You need me to open wide?"

God smiled, moved His left hand slightly and said, "Already taken care of, Jerry."

Sure enough, running my tongue over my teeth felt smoother than I could ever remember. "Thanks," I said. "But…"

"Let Me interrupt you for a change," God said, still smiling. "It's like this…I'm Me because I say I'm Me. I don't allow impostors here."

"Well, God, please forgive me for having such a suspicious mind," I continued, "But if You were an impostor, that's exactly the sort of thing You'd say. Isn't it?"

God folded one arm over another, and rested His chin on His upright arm. After a brief pause, He said, "I guess that's true enough,

Jerry. But…where exactly is this coming from? The last time we talked, you seemed as though you were learning to like it here. I showed you some things that you were quite happy to accept. But I leave you to yourself for a little while, and now you're not so sure. What happened?"

"God, I'd rather not say," I told Him, very softly, turning away my gaze. I still didn't want to get anyone in trouble!

"Who's been talking to you?" God asked, a little more insistently.

When I didn't answer, I could feel His look burning into me, so I glanced at Him. He looked into my eyes briefly. "Oh, you've met Olga."

I nearly fell down from shock. "You know about her?" I asked in astonishment.

God said, "Of course I do. This is My place, isn't it?" He said, a little impatiently.

"So who is she?"

"Oh…where do I begin? Let's just say that Olga is someone who doesn't know when she's well off. In life, she was very pious, but not very happy. Her standards for others were very high, and you know what that meant, of course."

God was apparently waiting for me to answer, so I took a moment to think of someone I'd known who'd been like that. Then it came to me; there was a woman in our church… "Ah, yes," I said to God. "She was constantly disappointed, wasn't she?"

I received an affirming smile for an answer. "Exactly. Even here," God explained, "She's not exactly thrilled. The sad thing is, she's not at all unique. There's never been a shortage of Olgas, I'm a little sorry to say."

We started drifting along with a gently zephyr that had sprung up. The Lord went on to say, "To tell you the truth, Jerry, I'd just as soon not have her sort around, but their piety has to have some reward, I suppose. So there you have it. Another example of how I maybe set the standards for admission lower than they should be. And now, she, and others like her, spend their eternity making others nervous," God said, very matter-of-factly.

"She's very good at it," I told Him. "She certainly unsettled me," I added, with a nervous laugh. "She even said she'd never met You."

"She really said that?" God asked, as one of His rather furry eyebrows moved like a caterpillar.

"Yes; why don't You ask her Yourself if You don't believe me?" I answered, for some reason still getting defensive when there was clearly no need to.

Apparently that didn't bother the Creator. "Oh, no need for that; I knew she *felt* that way, but I didn't realize until now that she was going around telling people that. Pity."

"Can it really be true?" I asked.

"Sort of true. To her mind, she hasn't really met Me," He said, rather sadly.

"How is that possible?" I wondered.

"Oh, it's like this," God said as He started His explanation. "Olga—and far too many others like her—have a sense that nobody is good enough for Me—especially themselves, of course. So when they get here, they're convinced that there's still some kind of ranking system, and they're just not high enough on the list. Too bad for them."

"But has she really not met You?" I wondered.

"Jerry, I make a point of seeing her all the time," God said. "Sometimes I'm a scruffy dog that snaps at her heels; I'm also the woman she meets for tea regularly; I'm even her gardener, for My sake. Once I even took the form of an oaf who stepped on her toes at a movie." God started to chuckle.

"What happened?"

"Good old Olga. She threatened to report Me."

"Report *You*? To who?" If there was a police force around here, I hadn't seen it.

"I have no idea," God said with a laugh. "I haven't been able to figure that one out. What a piece of work Olga is!"

"She's definitely…an eccentric," I said, barely able to keep myself from saying "nutcase" in front of God.

"Yes, I know," He replied, suddenly looking very thoughtful. "But at least she's no threat to anyone. I sometimes think she maybe just doesn't like it here very much."

"Is that even possible?"

"More than you'll ever know, Jerry."

"So why don't You do something about her?" I wondered.

"Do something about Olga? Why would I want to do that?" God asked in obvious astonishment.

Once again I noticed that faint odor of toast burning, which should have been my first clue that I'd said something irksome. "I don't know…maybe because she upsets people, in a place where they're not supposed to be upset?"

God was slowly growing larger, and darker. "I'm not sure I see your logic," He said curtly. "She's in her Heaven."

The sensation of foolishness had returned. "Well…" was all I managed to say.

Frowning in my direction, God threatened, "Why, perhaps, don't I do something about *you* instead?"

"Me! What have I done?" I was at the exact point where shock, indignation, and fear all meet.

God pointed one of His fingers directly between my eyes and said, "Maybe I have been giving you too much credit, Jerry. I thought I could trust you, so I've spent no small amount of effort to try and explain a few minor things to you. But the very first time—the *first time*—you encounter something that differs from My explanation to you, you're ready to toss your entire faith away. Haven't you learned anything?"

Despite the lurking sense that I was tiptoeing too near the rim of a volcano, a kernel of my doubt persisted.

Whether God was really real or just a very perceptive spirit was a question that remained unanswered in my mind, and He could sense it.

"I think you need to sort this out without Me," He said, unable or unwilling to mask his disappointment. "But while you're thinking, think about this: If you can't trust Me, here in My home, whom can you trust anywhere?"

And He disappeared.

CHAPTER 23

That last conversation with God—at least, I hoped it was Him—had disturbed my thinking in ways I could not have anticipated. What was His real nature?

Suddenly, it occurred to me that He had already given me all the answers I would ever need. It was in a knowledge that was beyond knowing—but never unknown.

It was like a confidence in a paradox; a paradoxical thought in itself. If it was simple, why would God bother to spend so much effort on me, one of a limitless number of His creations?

I floated around a bit, however long it took for me to sort through my thoughts, pondering not only God's apparent paradox, but about many other things—who I had been, and what I had been. But of course by this point, I knew that just having a well-formed question was enough to make God appear—and sure enough, there He was.

"Are you still angry with me?" I asked.

"Anger isn't the right word," was all He said. Still, He seemed a bit irritated as He asked, "What's on your mind this time, Jerry? Having another crisis of faith? Wondering if perhaps I'm real but you aren't?"

That took me by surprise. "I hadn't even thought of that," I told Him.

"Maybe you should," He said sternly.

"Thank You…I'll give it some thought. And it does kind of lead me to a question," I said.

"Which is?"

"Well, it's just that we've been told since childhood that You created us in Your image."

God laughed a little. "Well, that's one small—very small—part of it."

"What do you mean?" I asked.

He explained, "It's this whole concept of creation and image that you have."

I was puzzled. "How many kinds can there be?"

"Look at it this way. To you, perhaps you think you're in My image and I'm in yours. But you are hardly My only creation. To horses, I appear as one of them. Lobsters see Me with little pincers, and honeybees see Me as the Queen of All Queens. For every type of My creatures, I know that you're all more comfortable with the familiar. But keep this in mind, Jerry— I'm everybody's and everything's God, not just yours."

As God was explaining all this to me, His form rapidly shifted from creature to creature. As it was happening, I realized that I was changing too. Yet no matter what kind of creature I became, God was still God.

I had never thought of Divinity this way. "So what you're saying is…"

"Exactly. I have to listen not only to your prayers, but the prayers of the houseflies in your kitchen that pray you'll forget to clean off the stovetop. And to the spider that wants the housefly to get too close to the corner of the window. They don't have much of a consciousness—not by your selfish standards, anyway—but to Me, they make their pleas known clearly enough."

I shook my head with disbelief—sorry, poor choice of words. I was amazed at His infinite grace. "You have quite a balancing act to maintain," I said.

"Like nothing you can possibly imagine," God told me. "That little juggling act of mine that you saw earlier was nothing compared to what I'm really keeping up with. Some life forms are pretty demanding…and you'd be really shocked to learn just how many mice want you humans to simply go away. Frankly, I don't know if I can put them off forever."

"But You say in the Bible that man is Your favorite creature!" I protested.

"Jerry, this is obviously news to you, but the Bible was written by men who were interpreting My messages."

Before I could express my outrage, He went on. "If gerbils had written Scriptures, they might have placed themselves at the top of that list, yes?"

I calmed down as I thought for a bit. "I see what you mean," I admitted.

"But let Me ask you something, Jerry," He said, making sure I was paying attention. "What makes you think that there even is a list of My favorite creatures?"

I didn't know what to say.

"Relax, Jerry, I wasn't really expecting an answer. We'll talk some more about all this later," God informed me. "But just so you don't feel too bad, the Bible isn't the only case of men trying to control Me through their words."

"I'm sure there are plenty of examples," I said.

"Examples are everywhere," He replied, smiling slightly. "But let Me show you what they're up against."

Everything around me lost its color until I was surrounded by total darkness. Then, slowly, there was a gradual brightening, like the dawn of a clear morning. At first it was warm and reassuring; its presence was physical, like a warm gentle rain. Basking in it was a gentle reassurance.

But then the light grew more and more intense until it passed a point beyond which it wasn't pleasant anymore. The brightness began to feel like millions of tiny needles piercing every part of my body, on all sides. Soon I began to feel overwhelmed by the light, as though it had begun to consume me.

As the light absorbed me, just for an instant, I felt a violent shudder. Before I could react, an intrusion of everything broke in upon me. I saw and felt and smelled and tasted and *knew* everything, all at once. For the first time since I had arrived, I was scared. Panic began to grow as I became terrified, even more than when as a child I'd stuck my fingers in a lamp. It was simply horrifying to be so aware.

But beyond this terror was a far worse fright.

Adding to the pressure of the knowledge squeezing in on me from every direction and dimension was a far more intrusive sensation; a multitude of screaming desperation. Entreaties, questions, pleas, prayers, curses; hate, love, admiration, doubt, reverence, lives starting and lives ending, whirling around me and through me like a tornado, pulling me, tearing at me, insatiable and utterly relentless.

I felt madness swallowing me. I tried to find enough calm in my mind to search for somewhere to escape, but everywhere my thoughts turned, I found no comfort. There were only immense landscapes of fear. A shrieking, heartbreaking, desolate terror...so much *fear!* It struck me in the same instant and mixed with my own initial sense of horror to create a sensation of such unconquerable fright that I felt as though I would welcome madness, or a million deaths to this! The wishes and needs of every single creature in God's creation, all turning to me for answers, to me, to me alone! What did they all want? How could I ever even understand them all, and then begin to answer them?

To my ultimate fright, as my mind nearly shattered, I realized—there was nowhere I could turn for help.

Never before had I so urgently felt the need to run—but there was simply nowhere to go.

Just as I started to surrender to the idea that I couldn't take any more, the light quickly receded. Soon it had diminished to a soft green glow. God's merciful face appeared before me. I reached out and took Him by the hand.

Slowly the vortex in my mind subsided. "Please…please don't do that again," I whispered to God, breathless with a lingering terror that lurked just out of sight, threatening to return with renewed power.

But God's reassurance flowed through me, His peace melting the fear. Gently He said, "Jerry, you are safe. You are always safe with Me. I won't put you through that again, Jerry. You'll be all right now."

After I stopped shaking, God asked, "Are you feeling better?"

I nodded in an unsteady agreement.

"I'm sorry I had to do that," He said. "But I needed to make you see."

I still felt frail as a tall blade of grass, but managed to say, "I never knew it was possible to see too much." Most of the images were fading from my mind, and I welcomed their departure. Still, certain realizations still flashed in front of me, convulsing my mind and contributing to my sense of disorientation.

"Yes, now you know. I see many things that I wish I could simply avoid, but I don't always have that luxury," God said sadly.

"At first, I was enjoying the light," I told God. "It was beautiful. But it was just too much, and far too fast."

"A little of it was wonderful, though, wasn't it?" God asked. When I nodded in agreement, He went on, "If you ever think you're ready to try that again, I'll be more certain that you can handle it. But don't worry, it will be a while. Quite a while, in fact, despite all that you've learned since you arrived."

"Have I learned a great deal?" I asked, continuing my slow recovery.

God stopped for a moment and seemed lost in thought. "Let's put it this way—at least I've told you a lot…how much you've actually learned won't be clear right away," He replied.

I laughed to myself in agreement. "I feel as though I'm doing okay," I said.

God smiled His patient smile and said, "Yes, Jerry, you're off to a good start. If you ask Me, and I'm sure you're just about to, our getting acquainted is working out very well."

"Really?" I asked, feeling flattered. "You find that You actually like me?"

Chuckling, God placed His hands on my shoulders. "Jerry...these little talks of ours aren't about Me getting to know you. I created you, remember? I've known you forever, and can't forget anything about you. I've been putting this effort into all this so that you can get to know Me."

I felt a little ashamed of myself. "Of course, God. I guess I should have thought a little more before talking."

God sighed. "You and so many others, Jerry. But relax. Overall, I'm very pleased with you, if it doesn't embarrass you to hear that. For one thing, I hope you've just seen that being Me isn't as easy as it looks."

The horror of it still had not completely left me. "Yes...yes, I never took the effort to consider what all this must be like for You," I answered. "I saw the universe from such a small perspective. But I know now that there's so very much more to it."

"Better late than never, Jerry. Now, I just hope that I don't lose you."

"Lose me?" I wondered. "How could you lose me? Lose me to what?"

God leaned close and whispered, "Lose you to the *indifference of bliss*."

I shook my head in protest and said, "No! No...I just don't see how that could happen. Not after all this! In fact, I wish there were some way I could go back and teach the living about all that I know now."

Epilogue

Seeing God like that, burdened by responsibilities beyond my comprehension, gave me the idea to get all of this recorded.

Now that I've finished, I see that there's a brightly-colored garden off in the distance, far, far below me. The plants are singing to one another. It looks pretty interesting. I didn't know that plants could sing.

Maybe I'll investigate.

Or maybe not. After all, I feel pretty good right where I am.

Afterword

Several of those who have read drafts of this work have asked about my motivation in writing it.

The origin of this book dates to 1995, when I was going through a fairly difficult period. At the time, I had a series of dreams which featured many of the episodes that are recorded in this book.

Over the next few months, I started to write them down. I kept writing until they formed the book you have just read.

One reader reproached me by saying that this book is "not exactly orthodox," but frankly, that is the point. Its intention is not to be definitive, but rather speculative.

I have tried to resist the temptation to write a travelogue of Heaven; I don't really see the point of something like that—and the reactions I have received from several readers have convinced me that doing so would be rather futile anyway.

I guess we will all just have to wait and see for ourselves.

About the Author

Scott R. Lucado is an author with an unusual background.

Mr. Lucado never completed college; he felt he needed an education outside of what the academic world had to offer.

For the first year after leaving the University of Illinois at Chicago, he lived in a small apartment in a very rough neighborhood, often sleeping on the floor to avoid stray gunfire, and learning a great deal that wasn't taught in college.

In the late 1980's, he co-created a key technological breakthrough for creating a hybrid intelligent tutoring system, combining a rule-based expert system shell with an interactive multimedia delivery system. The publication of this work has become part of the standard bibliography of work on the uses of artificial intelligence for training and education.

In the late 1990's, Mr. Lucado pioneered the use of internet help-wanted ads as a means of gathering corporate intelligence, a technique that was featured in the Wall Street Journal.

Mr. Lucado's favorite authors, among others, include Leo Tolstoy, Friedrich Nietzsche, Patrick O'Brian, Barbara Tuchman, and John D. MacDonald. He hopes to be able to talk with them some day—but not too soon.

Mr. Lucado met the woman of his dreams in 1980, and married her in 1997. (Her dreams were a little different for a while.) They live in their adopted hometown in Texas.

0-595-23559-X